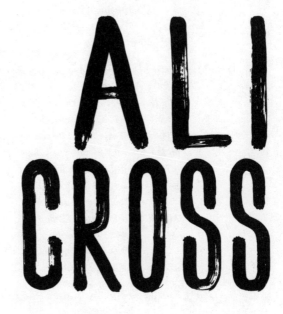

JIMMY PATTERSON BOOKS FOR YOUNG READERS

James Patterson Presents

Sci-Fi Junior High by John Martin and Scott Seegert

Sci-Fi Junior High: Crash Landing by John Martin and Scott Seegert

How to Be a Supervillain by Michael Fry

How to Be a Supervillain: Born to Be Good by Michael Fry

How to Be a Supervillain: Bad Guys Finish First by Michael Fry

The Unflushables by Ron Bates

Ernestine, Catastrophe Queen by Merrill Wyatt

Scouts by Shannon Greenland

The Middle School Series by James Patterson

Middle School, The Worst Years of My Life

Middle School: Get Me Out of Here!

Middle School: Big Fat Liar

Middle School: How I Survived Bullies, Broccoli, and Snake Hill

Middle School: Ultimate Showdown

Middle School: Save Rafe!

Middle School: Just My Rotten Luck

Middle School: Dog's Best Friend

Middle School: Escape to Australia

Middle School: From Hero to Zero

Middle School: Born to Rock

Middle School: Here Comes Trouble

The I Funny Series by James Patterson

I Funny

I Even Funnier

I Totally Funniest

I Funny TV

I Funny: School of Laughs

The Nerdiest, Wimpiest, Dorkiest I Funny Ever

The Treasure Hunters Series by James Patterson

Treasure Hunters

Treasure Hunters: Danger Down the Nile

Treasure Hunters: Secret of the Forbidden City

For exclusives, trailers, and other information, visit jimmypatterson.org.

JAMES PATTERSON

ALI CROSS

JIMMY Patterson Books
Little, Brown and Company
New York Boston London

Copyright © 2019 by James Patterson

Hachette Book Group supports the right to free expression and the value of copyright. The purpose of copyright is to encourage writers and artists to produce the creative works that enrich our culture.

The scanning, uploading, and distribution of this book without permission is a theft of the author's intellectual property. If you would like permission to use material from the book (other than for review purposes), please contact permissions@hbgusa.com. Thank you for your support of the author's rights.

JIMMY Patterson Books / Little, Brown and Company
Hachette Book Group
1290 Avenue of the Americas, New York, NY 10104
JamesPatterson.com

First Edition: November 2019

JIMMY Patterson Books is an imprint of Little, Brown and Company, a division of Hachette Book Group, Inc. The Little, Brown name and logo are trademarks of Hachette Book Group, Inc. The JIMMY Patterson Books® name and logo are trademarks of JBP Business, LLC.

The publisher is not responsible for websites (or their content) that are not owned by the publisher.

The Hachette Speakers Bureau provides a wide range of authors for speaking events. To find out more, go to hachettespeakersbureau.com or call (866) 376-6591.

Cataloging-in-publication data is available at the Library of Congress.

ISBN (hc) 978-0-316-53041-5; (large print) 978-0-316-42634-3

10 9 8 7 6 5 4 3 2 1

LSC-C

Printed in the United States of America

ALI
CROSS

CHAPTER 1

IT HAD BEEN three days since my friend disappeared and I was starting to think the worst might have happened.

The last time I'd seen him was on Friday, December 21st, just after 3:30 p.m. That was on the sidewalk in front of Washington Latin Middle School where Gabe and I were in the same class. We'd just gotten out for winter break, and as far as I was concerned, I knew exactly how we were going to kick it off.

"So I'll see you tonight at seven," I'd said. The plan was to get online with our usual crew and start a marathon session of *Outpost*, our favorite game.

"Just try and stop me," Gabe had joked.

That was it. Then he'd turned east on E Street and started walking home. I'd turned west and done the same. I didn't even think about it. Why would I? Who ever thinks, "maybe that's the last time I'll ever see my friend"?

But Gabe never did make it home that day. He wasn't picking up his phone, and he hadn't answered any of the half-million texts I'd sent him, either. Now it was Christmas Eve. Three days had gone by, and it was like Gabe had just disappeared.

Except, see, that's the thing. People don't just disappear. There's always an explanation. That's what my dad says, and he should know. His name is Alex Cross. He's a homicide detective with the Washington DC police, and I'll tell you this much: I hope I can be half the detective he is someday.

In the meantime, I couldn't stop thinking about Gabe. Couldn't stop wondering what had happened to him. Couldn't stop a whole lot of really bad thoughts from passing through my brain, like one scary movie after another.

In fact, if anyone had asked me, I would have told them there was only one thing I wanted for Christmas that year. I wanted Gabe Qualls to be found.

And I mean alive.

CHAPTER 2

"ALI? COME ON, little brother. Heads up. You're on."

"Say what?"

I guess I got lost in my own thoughts for a second there. It happens all the time. We were in church for Christmas Eve services. I looked around and realized my older brother, Damon, wasn't the only one giving me the eyeball. St. Anthony's Church was packed, and I guess Father Bernadin had already introduced me while I was sitting there spacing out.

"Let's try that again," Father Bernadin said in

his Haitian accent, and with a kind of impatient smile aimed my way. "The annual Christmas Eve children's prayer will be led by our own Ali Cross tonight. Ali, would you like to come up?"

The pastor moved aside for me as I stepped up to the old wooden lectern and looked out at the congregation, a whole sea of black faces like mine. Something like four hundred pairs of eyes looked back, waiting for me to get my act together.

It's supposed to be a big deal to get chosen for the children's prayer at my church, especially on Christmas Eve. I guess you could say it was an honor. But my mind was like mush that night, and I was wishing they'd tapped someone else.

"Go ahead, son," Dad said from the front row. He pointed at the page in my hand where I had the whole prayer written out, since I didn't trust myself to remember it by heart.

When I looked at the words on that paper, it was like they didn't mean much. Not compared to being alone out there on the street, or kidnapped, or whatever else Gabe might have been going through.

I hadn't known him that long—only since the

beginning of middle school. But we got to be friends right away. I saw him in the cafeteria one day, eating by himself and working on a pretty cool drawing. I mentioned something about it, and that's when I found out he was a total *Outpost* fan, like me. Ever since then, we'd been gaming together, he'd come over to watch movies, and that kind of thing. But he never talked about himself much, and I never really asked. Now I was thinking maybe I should have.

Like I also should have just read the prayer anyway and gotten it over with like I was supposed to. But I couldn't.

"I know this is usually a prayer for kids everywhere, but if it's okay, I'd like to pray for just one kid tonight," I said. "A lot of you know Gabriel Qualls. He's in my grade at Washington Latin. He doesn't really come to church, but the point is, he's been missing for three days."

I thought Father Bernadin might cut me off right there, but he didn't. Everyone just waited, so I kept going.

"When I was working on this prayer, I thought a lot about the night Jesus was born, and how nobody wanted to make any room for him, and how he had to be born in a stable," I said. "So now I'm wondering if maybe we could learn something from that. I'm hoping we can all make room for Gabe. Like in our hearts. And in our prayers."

I didn't know if this was going to help, but I figured it couldn't hurt. How often do you get the chance to send four hundred prayers someone's way, all at once? My voice was kind of shaky, but I just kept talking.

"Dear God," I said, and everyone went still. Most of the congregation bowed their heads. "I know you know where Gabriel Qualls is. And I know you probably have a plan for him, just like you do for anyone else. I don't want to ask too much, but if you're listening, please watch out for Gabe tonight. Please help bring him home again soon. And, um... I guess that's all. In Jesus's name, amen."

"Amen!" the congregation echoed back at me.

Then, just before I stepped down, I realized there was one more thing.

"Oh, and happy birthday, Jesus," I said.

Because hey, it *was* Christmas, after all.

CHAPTER 3

MAYBE I SHOULD have said a prayer for my dad, too. Because I wasn't the only one dealing with some heavy stuff that night.

In fact, when we came out of church after services, there was a crowd of people with cameras and microphones waiting for us. It was a little like walking into a pack of hungry lions—and guess who was on the menu?

"Detective Cross! Care to comment on the assault charges against you?"

"Alex, over here! Is there a trial date set?"

"They're saying you need to go to jail, Detective Cross, do you agree?"

It was all just words. I knew that. But at the same time, it's not true what people say about words. They *can* hurt you. And all those questions the reporters were throwing at my dad felt like they might as well have been throwing rocks.

Here's what it was all about. Six months ago, Dad had gone to interview the father of a murder suspect. The suspect's name was Tyler Yang, and he was already in jail. But when Dad got to the Yangs' house that day, Mr. Yang wasn't having it. He said his son was innocent and tried to kick Dad off their front porch. It turned into a scuffle. Then Mr. Yang fell down the steps. His head hit the pavement really hard, and he had to go to the hospital. Ever since then, he'd been in a coma.

Now the Yang family was suing Dad and the police department for assault. Maybe also for murder, depending on whether Mr. Yang survived.

It was crazy. I didn't believe Dad was guilty for a second—he said it was an accident. But try telling that to the crowd following us up the street that night. The closer Dad's trial got, the more they were dogging him with nonstop questions everywhere he went.

"Alex, did you deliberately push Mr. Yang down the stairs?"

"Are you ashamed of yourself, Detective Cross?"

"What's it feel like to put someone in the hospital?"

My stepmom, Bree, grabbed my hand. I took my great-grandma, Nana Mama, by the arm on the other side. I wanted these people out of my face. I wished I had some kind of flashbang on me, the kind they use for police raids. Not to hurt anyone, but just loud and disorienting enough to make these reporters wish they'd all stayed home on Christmas Eve.

Meanwhile, we still had to get back to the car.

"Detective Cross, do you think you set a good example for your family?" someone asked.

A spotlight hit my eyes then, and another camera popped up, pointing right at me and my sister. That's when I heard Jannie let out a sob. And even though I'm the youngest, I wasn't going to let them do that to her. Or to anyone in my family.

"Hey! Back off!" I shouted. "My dad didn't do anything! So why are you coming for him like this? In case you hadn't noticed, it's supposed to be Christmas."

"Shh," Bree said in my ear. "Just keep walking."

"Ali? Anything else to say?" another reporter asked. "Are you proud of your dad?"

"You proud of yours?" I asked.

Then I felt Dad's hand on my shoulder.

"Not another word," he said.

But I couldn't help it. Sometimes my mouth starts going and I can't find the off switch.

"Yeah, I'm proud of my dad!" I yelled back. "Why don't you put *that* in your story? Or better yet, why don't you write something about Gabriel Qualls, and do some good for a change?"

I shouldn't have said that last part about doing good. Dad's always reminding me, we have freedom of speech here, and freedom of the press, too. Just because a few reporters don't know how to be professional, it doesn't mean they're all bad. They're mostly good at their jobs. Just like cops.

"Who's Gabriel Qualls, Ali?" one of the reporters shouted.

"Is he a friend of yours?"

"What's the story there?"

But I didn't get to answer. Dad was already stepping in to take over. Which was just as well, because I was ready to go *off* on these people.

And trust me, nobody needed that.

ALEX CROSS

DETECTIVE ALEX CROSS looked at his son Ali and tried not to smile. There was nothing funny about what was going on, but it was hard not to admire a fire that big, burning that brightly, in a guy as little as Ali. He had as much spirit as the person he was nicknamed for—the greatest boxer of all time, Muhammad Ali.

Meanwhile, these reporters weren't going to leave them alone until they got some kind of comment. There was even a chance one or more would follow the family back home if Alex stayed silent.

So he stepped forward and raised his voice above the fray.

"As you all know perfectly well, I can't discuss my case here," Alex said. "If you want to hear any more about it, I suggest you come to my trial and take careful notes."

"Detective Cross, can you say a little more about—" Russ Miller from Channel Four started in, but Alex spoke right over him.

"However," he said, "let me make one thing very clear. None of this has anything to do with my family. My children will have nothing more to say about the matter, tonight or *ever.* Understood?"

Alex glanced down at Ali, just to make sure he was listening, too. The reporters started in with another firestorm of questions, but Alex was done.

"That's all I have to say," he told the crowd. "Thank you, good night, and Merry Christmas to you all."

Then with a papa bear's sweep of his arm, he pointed the way for Bree, Nana Mama, Damon, Jannie, and Ali to follow him back to the car.

Enough was enough. It was time to go home.

CHAPTER 4

I GOT A real talking to in the car on the way home.
Not from Dad or Bree. From Nana Mama.

"You need to check yourself, young man," Nana
told me. "What exactly was that supposed to be
back there?"

"Did you hear what those reporters were saying?" I asked. "They made Jannie cry."

"I can take care of myself," Jannie said.

"That's not the point," Nana said. "Why do you
think they speak that way?"

"To get us to answer their questions," I said.

"More than that, they want your father to get mad," Nana Mama said. "They want him to behave exactly like the angry and violent man he's accused of being. And you know Alex would do *anything* to defend you, including putting himself in harm's way. So why don't you think twice next time you feel like taking things into your own hands?"

Nana Mama is ninety-something years old, but she can still get fired up. And believe me, when she does, you feel the heat.

"I'm sorry, Dad," I said. I really was. I felt like a dummy for falling into that trap.

"I know this isn't easy on you guys," Dad said. "But Nana's right."

"When they go low..." Bree said.

"We go high," I said, along with Damon and Jannie. It was one of Bree's favorite quotes, but to be honest, it was getting kind of old. I mean, all those grown-ups were out there being a bunch of jerks and *I* was the one who had to do the right thing?

"In any case," Bree said, "that was a beautiful thing you did in church, Ali."

"Yes," Nana Mama agreed. "Sending all those prayers up for Gabriel can only do him good."

I was glad to get back on Nana Mama's good side, anyway. And now that Gabe had come up again, I had some questions.

"Hey, Dad?" I asked from the back. "Have you heard anything new about his case?"

"Nothing since you asked me this afternoon," Dad said. "I know you're anxious, son, but I won't be able to check in with Detective Sutter until after tomorrow."

Detective Wendy Sutter was the police officer assigned to Gabe's case. That much, I knew. But there hadn't been any word on how it was going, or if it was going at all.

"Don't worry *too* much, sweetie," Bree told me. "MPD closes ninety-nine percent of its missing persons cases."

"I know," I said. But I was still going to worry. I mean, someone had to be part of the other 1 percent. What if that was Gabe? What if he was never found?

I couldn't stop turning it all over in my mind.

That's just the way my brain works, like a generator in a blackout, never stopping, always running, always going.

Meanwhile, I kept my mouth shut and rode the rest of the way home in silence, trying not to think about it too much, but thinking about it anyway.

Merry Christmas, Gabe. Wherever you are.

CHAPTER 5

IT SEEMED LIKE we'd had our share of bad news for one Christmas Eve, but when we got home there was more.

A lot more.

Bree parked the car in the garage, and we all headed across the backyard to get inside. Damon was walking ahead of everyone else, but then he stopped short.

"Dad?" he asked.

I looked where Damon was pointing, and saw

that one of the little windowpanes in our back porch door was broken. Then I noticed the door was open, too.

For a second, nobody said anything. I stood perfectly still, like I was frozen on the outside while everything sped up on the inside. Someone had definitely busted into our house.

"Wait here," Dad said.

"What's going on?" I asked.

"Just wait," he said.

Bree put a hand around my shoulder and pulled me closer while I kept my eyes glued to the back door. I didn't even know she'd called 911 until I heard her talking to the dispatcher.

"Hello, this is MPD Chief of Detectives, Brianna Stone," she said. Bree's my stepmom, which is why I call her Bree, but she's also a cop like my dad. "I'm off duty and unarmed, requesting a uniformed patrol at my house right away on a possible break-in. We'll need two units, one in front and one in the back alley."

While Dad moved toward the porch, I started scanning the ground around me. It was too dark to see footprints, if there were any. My guess was that someone had come in from the alley and over the garage roof.

I could just see it in my mind—a dark shadow of a bad guy, scaling his way up, over, and onto our property. Then across the yard, hugging the fence where the light from the alley wouldn't give him away. A quick punch through the back door glass with a gloved hand was all it would take. Then a careful reach inside, past the sharp edges. A turn of the knob—

And into the house.

Our house.

The question was—could he still be in there? And what was Dad walking into? As much as I want to be a real investigator someday, I don't know if I'd ever have the guts to do what he was doing just then. My heartbeat had already kicked into high gear, but it doubled down again as I watched Dad slowly push open the back door and disappear inside.

All we could do now was wait.

ALEX CROSS

ALEX CROSS STEPPED through the back door and onto the sunporch of his house. A bulb from the stovetop in the kitchen offered just enough light to see by. The porch was littered with winter boots and coats, as well as the old upright piano he sometimes played. Other than the broken back door glass, everything looked the same as it had when they'd left for church that night.

He stopped and listened for a creak, a footstep, or any indication that someone was still inside. Everyone always thought cops knew how not to be afraid in these situations, but it wasn't like that. He was scared, all right. He just couldn't let the fear stop him.

"Police!" he yelled.

His heart thumped out a ragged rhythm as he listened again, but the old house only answered with more silence.

Pushing on, Alex passed slowly through the kitchen and into the hall. When he reached the living room, he saw the floor around the Christmas tree was littered with crumpled paper, ribbon, and opened packages. Someone had torn through everything and almost certainly stolen the more valuable items. So much for Ali's brand-new laptop, along with whatever else had been taken.

Scumbags.

When Alex's phone vibrated, he looked down to see Bree's name on the screen.

"What's up?" he answered.

"Dispatch is sending two units," she said. "What's going on in there?"

"Some kind of robbery," he told her. "I think they're gone, but—"

He stopped short at the sound of an old window frame creaking open. Whoever had broken into the house was somewhere upstairs, trying to make a quick escape from the sound of it.

"Hang on!" he told her.

He launched up the steps, three at a time. When he got to the upstairs hallway, there was nothing more to hear, but an unmistakable cold breeze was blowing down the hall from the direction of his own bedroom.

Three fast strides brought him into the room. Two more and he was at the open window, pushing past the blowing curtains to scan the scene outside.

The gutter on the front porch roof had been torn off. Other than that, there was no sign of anyone. The street looked deserted, and whoever had just been here was gone now.

"Alex?" Bree's voice came over the phone. "Alex! What's going on?"

"I'm here," he said. "We just missed them."

"Them?"

"Him, her, them, I don't know," he said, flipping

on a light. "Whoever it was, they went through all the gifts under the tree and..."

Again, Alex stopped short. His bedroom was a disaster. Dresser drawers hung open. Clothes were everywhere. The mattress was overturned, and a lamp lay in pieces on the floor.

But none of that was the worst news.

"Bree, we've got a bigger problem here," he said.

"What is it?" she asked.

"I'm up in our room right now. They went through everything. Including the nightstands," he told her.

"Oh...no," she said.

"Yeah. Both lockboxes are gone, and both of our police weapons along with them."

The whole thing had just jumped up a level. Anyone with the right tools would be able to pop those lockboxes in no time. The boxes were meant as a home safety measure, nothing more than that.

This was no longer a simple robbery. Now there were two firearms out there on the street. Two police weapons in the wrong hands.

"Don't mention the guns to the kids," he added.

"I won't," she said.

Ali, Jannie, and Damon knew exactly what was in those lockboxes, but it wouldn't help anything to talk about it now. Their Christmas Eve was already a disaster. No sense making it worse.

If that was even possible.

CHAPTER 6

ONCE THE POLICE got to our house, we had to wait
in the kitchen for a long time. Uniformed officers
came through first, then a team of crime scene
techs and Detective Olayinka, who went over the
whole place with Dad and Bree. This was all 100
percent serious, but it was also just like something
out of an episode of *Law & Order*. I'll watch old
repeats of that show any chance I get. So yeah, my
radar was definitely on high that night, sucking up
every detail.

The good news was, everyone was okay. The bad news was, all our presents had been stolen, including the laptop I wasn't supposed to know I was getting for Christmas. That was a real bummer, but I didn't have to be a detective to know that now wasn't the time to go whining to Dad about it.

Because something else was going on. Detective Olayinka spent an extra-long time with Dad and Bree upstairs while the crime scene techs worked in the living room. I didn't know what they were talking about up there, but you could just *tell* there was some kind of secret in the air.

Or, at least, I could tell. I wasn't sure if Jannie and Damon had picked up on it.

"Weirdest Christmas ever," Jannie said. It was way past midnight by now and her chin was practically on the table. They hadn't brought up their missing presents, either. We all knew this was serious. We just couldn't do anything about it.

"Do you think it was one of those people who've been trashing Dad so bad lately?" Damon asked.

"Could be," Jannie said. "I mean, it's not like a

secret where we live. And Dad's got more than his share of people coming down on him lately."

"We all do," Damon said.

"What do you mean?" I asked.

"It's like for some people, 'Cross' is a dirty word now," Damon said. "You know. For anyone who thinks Dad's guilty."

"Guilty of what, though?" I asked. "He didn't do anything. I mean, I feel bad that Mr. Yang fell down those stairs, but it was an accident."

"You don't have to tell me that," Damon said. "Tell it to all those people who think Dad pushed him. Or assaulted him. Or both."

None of this was making me feel any better. But Damon was right. Those reporters outside the church weren't the only ones giving Dad grief about his trial. Regular people were saying all kinds of messed-up stuff about him, too. I know there are a lot of valid reasons people are talking about police brutality these days. Dad knows it, too. There have been way too many problems with it in the past few years, and it brings down the whole community when a police officer abuses their power. For Dad, it's made this case more complicated. I'd seen a ton of people accusing my dad of terrible stuff online and it was hard to take, even though I knew my Dad would never do those things.

I'd seen it all online, even though I wasn't supposed to be reading it.

Either way, I didn't want to just sit there talking anymore. This break-in was the last thing Dad needed right now, with his trial and the real chance that he could go to jail for something that wasn't his fault. He might not be a detective much longer, which is all I ever wanted to be. The best, like him.

I jerked back from the table, my chair scraping loudly on the floor. I wanted to get a look at the crime scene.

I wanted to *investigate* this thing.

"Where are you going?" Nana asked when I got up from the table.

"Just to the bathroom," I said, and slipped out of the kitchen before she decided to stop me.

When I got to the living room, the crime scene techs were there, wearing blue gloves and head-lamps, along with black sweatshirts that said ERT on the back in big white letters. The Evidence Response Team. They find all the clues—visible and invisible—that the perpetrators leave behind at a crime scene, then figure out exactly what they mean, like solving a riddle. That's always seemed like a cool job to me.

"Hey, little dude, you supposed to be in here?" one of the guys asked. He was carrying a camera. The other one was working a handheld blacklight, going over every inch of the room. No wonder it was taking so long.

"I'm good," I said with a smile, like that answered the question. "What are you looking for, exactly?"

"Fingerprints, mostly, and any other trace evidence," he said.

"Find anything?"

The guy smiled. "I don't think I'm supposed to talk to you about this," he said. "Sorry about your Christmas, though."

"It's okay," I said. It really was. A lot of people had it way worse than us. Including Gabe, I was guessing. And as long as I was standing there, I figured it couldn't hurt to try another angle with this guy.

"Can I ask you something else?" I said.

"Depends on what it's about," he told me.

"Let's say you were looking for a missing person," I said. "Someone who had disappeared, like, three days ago. What would you do about it?"

The guy nodded, and it seemed like he really thought for a second. I liked how he wasn't treating me like a kid.

"Well, I'm no detective. I'm just a tech," he said. "But if it were me, I'd get it up on the MPD missing persons page. Also, any neighborhood Facebook pages where they track this stuff. Social media can be your best friend in a case like that. But you need feet on the ground, too."

"What does that mean?" I asked.

"I'd comb the neighborhood, working out from wherever the missing person was last seen. Maybe get a team knocking on doors, handing out flyers, that kind of thing."

I had about a million more questions, but that's as far as I got.

"Ali?" Dad yelled from upstairs. "What are you doing down there?"

"Just going to the bathroom," I answered.

The crime scene guy smiled, but he didn't bust me. "He's no bother!" the guy said, as Dad came down the stairs.

"Oh, yes he is," Dad said. "Trust me. This kid's never seen a Sherlock Holmes story or a cop show on TV that he didn't soak up like a sponge."

That was true. Like I said, I wanted to be a detective so I couldn't get enough of anything with a mystery or a crime. I also like books by Walter Mosley, Blue Balliett, Trenton Lee Stewart, Varian Johnson, Agatha Christie, and a bunch of others.

But I didn't want to look like a geek in front of the investigators, so I didn't say all that out loud.

"In any case," Dad told me, "you can head up to bed. We're done up there, and it's time to get some sleep. Tomorrow is still Christmas, after all."

"Well, not exactly," I told him.

"Excuse me?" Dad asked.

I pointed over at the clock on the hall table. It was just after one in the morning by now.

"It's already Christmas," I said.

It was supposed to be one of the happiest days of the year. It goes to show how distracted we were that none of us noticed until now. Like Jannie said...

Weirdest Christmas ever.

CHAPTER 7

I DIDN'T STAY in bed for long. First, someone had been in our house, in this very room, looking through all my things. Maybe even sat on the bed I'm lying in now. It shook me up more than I wanted to admit, and even living with two cops didn't make me feel completely safe anymore.

Then there was the investigation. How was I going to sleep with about eight hundred different things running around inside my head?

Basically, I had three ideas about why someone might have done this.

One: It was one of those people who had already decided Dad was a dirty cop.

Two: It was just some random burglary, the kind that happens all the time, everywhere.

Three: It had something to do with Gabe. I know that sounds crazy, and I didn't even know what the connection might be, but it just seemed like a pretty big coincidence that this happened three days after he disappeared without a trace. Maybe he was kidnapped by the same people who robbed our house. Or maybe Gabe was even involved some-how. Dad always told me never to rule out possible connections.

I shook my head. The Gabe I knew was a good kid. He'd never so much as lied about anything, so the idea of him doing this was a definite long shot. If it *was* true, it'd have to be for a really desperate reason. Meanwhile, it was coming up on two in the morn-ing, but Dad and Bree were still downstairs. A second detective had shown up and they were all talking in low voices. Whatever their secret was, it had to be something big, and the longer it went on, the more I wanted to know what it was. I got out of bed and snuck into the hall to see what I could find out.

In my house, there are a few secrets only I know. Like, for instance, if you stick to the left side of our stairs and put your weight on the banister, you can keep them from creaking the whole way down. And then, if you sit on the fifth step from the bottom, you can hear what people are saying in the living room without anyone knowing you're there.

And what I heard next blew my mind.

"Did you already call this in to the desk sergeant?" Detective Olayinka asked.

"Yeah," Dad said. "Reported and registered."

"You said it was a Glock 19 and a Glock 22, is that right?" the new detective asked.

"That's right," Bree answered. "Alex still carries a .19. The .22 is mine. They were both secured, but it wouldn't take much to get inside those lockboxes with the right tools."

Now my head was spinning. Whoever had robbed us hadn't just gotten away with a few electronics. They'd stolen two guns, too. *Police weapons.*

Which was even less like Gabe than ever. I could barely imagine him breaking into a house, much less carrying around a couple of real Glocks.

"And now they're out on the street somewhere," Dad said. "God only knows what'll happen to them next."

"Don't beat yourself up about it," Detective Olayinka told him. "It's not like you were going to bring your duty weapons to church."

"Even so, this will be public information by tomorrow," Dad went on. "Somebody's bound to pick up on it. I've got more reporters on my butt these days than a dog has fleas."

I didn't mean to laugh at that, but Dad caught me off guard. It was just a little laugh, but enough to bust me if I wasn't careful. So I stayed low and started back up the stairs as stealthily as I could go. Then, when I heard Dad get up and start coming my way, I turned around like I was just headed down for the first time. Smooth, I know.

"Dude!" he said when he saw me. "You're supposed to be in bed."

"I can't sleep," I told him.

"It's Christmas."

"Exactly, Dad."

He just smiled at that. I think maybe he was taking it easy on me, with the robbery and everything that had happened.

"Just tell me what's going on," I said.

"Don't you worry about it."

"Come on, Dad. There must be something you can tell me." I didn't mention the guns, because I didn't want him to know how much I'd heard.

Dad took a deep breath. Then he came halfway up the stairs, met me in the middle, and we sat down right there.

"Here's as much as I'll say," he told me. "Our house wasn't the only one that got hit tonight. There were four other break-ins around the neighborhood."

I don't know what I was expecting to hear, but it wasn't that. Again, my mind went right back to Gabe. Could he have done all this? Not likely, but not impossible. Some part of me hoped there was a chance, anyway. At least then it would mean he was still around and that something even worse hadn't happened to him.

At the same time, it also meant this probably wasn't done by one of those random people who hated Dad so much for what happened with Mr. Yang. Otherwise, it would have just been our house that got robbed and not a whole string of them. That was worth something, anyway.

"Is there any kind of pattern to the break-ins?" I asked. The first thing they do with this kind of case is look for patterns, like if the robber had gone in through the back at every house, or stolen the same kind of stuff each time.

"That's all you're getting," Dad said. "Now scoot."

"Where were the other houses?" I asked. "Was it anyone we know?"

"Good night, Ali."

"Dad—" I tried again.

"Ali!" he said. He'd just switched over to his *enough* voice, which is basically like the sound of a big red stop sign. I knew I wasn't getting any more after that, so I said good night and took myself back to bed. Not that I expected to get any sleep.

I opened my copy of *The Parker Inheritance* to read for a while, but I just stared at the pages instead. I was too caught up putting all these different pieces together.

And I was starting to realize something. Between Dad's trial, and the break-in at our house, and the stolen police weapons, he was going to have less time to think about Gabe's case than ever before. Bree, too.

In other words, this was on me now. Not that I thought I could out-cop the cops. But if I didn't at least try, and then if something really bad happened to Gabe, I was going to wonder for the rest of my life if there was something I could have done.

I didn't just want to help anymore. Now I *needed* to.

Whatever it took.

ALEX CROSS

AFTER THE DETECTIVES went home and Bree took herself to bed, Alex Cross trudged up to his office in the attic. There was no sense trying to sleep that night. Might as well try to get a few things done, he thought.

Sitting at his desktop computer, Alex surfed around for the latest coverage on his upcoming trial. A quick Google search turned up page after page of results. Most of it was accurate enough, but it was easy to find plenty of lies and misinformation, too.

The worst of it, as usual, came from a blog called C.O.P., which stood for Call Out the Police. It was a site exclusively focused on police officers who had been accused of crimes themselves. So far, nobody had come after Alex harder than they had. There was no story about the stolen guns yet, but they'd already posted a video from outside St. Anthony's Church that night. The headline read, "Detective Cross Has Christmas Eve Meltdown in Front of Family."

The story that followed was as nasty as the headline itself. Alex gripped the edge of his desk as he read through, just to keep from throwing his computer right out the window.

His real concern, though, was the kids. Alex could take whatever the press wanted to throw at him, but there was no way to protect Ali, Jannie, and Damon from all of it. What was he going to do—erase the Internet?

Ali, especially, would be all over this. He was probably lying awake right now, looking at the same online trash his old man was reading one floor up. It hurt Alex in his heart, just thinking about it.

And it wasn't just *his* kids getting knocked around, either. Two families had been affected by the accident, in two very different ways. If Alex's trial didn't go well, he could be looking at jail time. But at least the Crosses were all together under one roof for now. It was the Yangs whose holiday had truly been ruined. Stanley Yang lay in a coma at Washington VA Medical Center that night, while his son, Tyler, was being held without bail at the DC Central Detention Facility. That put the rest of the Yangs at home on Christmas Eve, wondering when—or if—they'd ever be a whole family again.

There wasn't much Alex could do about that, but he did have one thing in mind. In fact, it had already been set in motion. Alex didn't really care if it got him into hot water.

And as soon as the sun started to come up, he put his plan into action.

ALEX CROSS

IT WAS 6:25 AM when John Sampson's text came through.

SAMPSON: Almost there. You ready for me?

CROSS: Be right there.

Sampson was Alex's best friend since way back in the day. He was also a fellow cop and, at the moment, a volunteer Christmas elf. Even if he did top out at six foot nine.

Alex tiptoed down to the front door where he let himself out into the crisp December morning.

He opened the car trunk and took out a heavy red cloth bag, stuffed with gifts, slinging it over his back, Santa-style.

"Ho, ho, ho! Merry Christmas, bud," Sampson called from his black Explorer as he pulled up to the curb.

"You, too," Alex answered. He dropped the red bag into Sampson's backseat, then opened the passenger door and got in.

"You're coming?" Sampson asked. "I thought you were going to hang back."

"I need to see this through," Alex said. "It's been a rough night."

"All right then," Sampson answered. "Let's put this sleigh in gear."

As they drove the quiet city streets from the Capitol Hill section of Southeast DC toward the Yangs' Northeast DC neighborhood, Alex filled his friend in on the break-in, the neighborhood robberies, and the stolen weapons from his house.

Sampson gave a low whistle. "Some Christmas," he said. "I'm really sorry, man."

"It's mostly the kids I'm worried about," Alex told

him. "Damon's confused. Jannie's afraid of all the people coming down on me lately. And Ali's got this friend who's gone missing, on top of everything else."

"You talking about the Qualls kid?" Sampson asked.

"That's right. Gabriel," Alex answered. "Ali's pretty down about it, but he also tends to get a little obsessive."

"That kid's gonna run the world one of these days," Sampson said with a dark smile. "I get tired just thinking about how fast his brain runs."

It was true, Alex thought. For better or worse, Ali's mind was always running, always firing on every cylinder. He was an intelligent, creative kid, but he also tended to fixate on whatever was in front of him, at which point he was more pit bull than wise old owl. That came with a tendency to make over-confident and sometimes rash decisions, which was the part that worried Alex the most.

"Here we are," Sampson said, coming to a stop on North Capitol Street. As per the plan, he'd parked several doors down from the Yang family's home. "You want me to ring the bell? Or just drop the goodies and run?"

"See if you can hear anyone inside first," Alex said. "Then do whatever makes sense."

Sampson hopped out and pulled the Santa sack from the backseat. Inside the bag were toys, clothes, a huge box of Christmas candy, and gift cards for Walmart and Safeway. It wasn't going to change anyone's life, but it was something, anyway.

As Alex watched, Sampson carried the bag up to the Yangs' front porch. He paused there for a second, listening, then rang the bell and hurried back down toward the car.

Alex slouched a little deeper in his seat. He didn't want to be seen here. He just wanted to see.

A second later, eight-year-old Leighanne Yang opened the front door. She was adorable in pale-yellow pajamas and a pair of red and gold bunny ears. When she saw the bag waiting on the porch, her eyebrows knit together in confusion. But as soon as she'd yanked it open to look inside, her face lit up like a Christmas tree.

"Mama! Grandma!" the girl shouted. "Santa came!"

And for the first time that Christmas, Alex Cross smiled.

CHAPTER 8

ON CHRISTMAS NIGHT, Nana and I had leftover turkey and cranberry sandwiches and stayed up late watching the Wizards–Knicks game. We're both Wizards fanatics—and Knicks haters—so it bummed us out when the New Yorkers won.

"I hate to say it," Nana complained, "but that sucked. Now, Ali, you forget I ever said that."

I forced myself not to laugh out loud. "Said what?"

The next morning, my dad woke me up before

7:00 a.m. I groaned, "Seriously? Seven o'clock? On my vacation? Why?"

"Seriously. Seven o'clock. Because I can. Besides, you're too young to need a vacation," Dad told me.

Anyway, it turned out great. We had breakfast at Armando's. It's a huge, special deal for me to eat out with Dad, just the two of us. Armando's has the best pancakes with strawberries and peaches and that's what I had. Dad had a big platter of huevos rancheros.

When we finished and I was groaning from happiness and an overfull belly, Dad dropped a little bomb on me. "We're going to go meet with Detective Sutter about Gabe. Ali, I want you to do a whole lot of listening and not much talking. She's the detective, not you. We clear?"

I sat up right away. "We're clear. We're good. We're great. And thank you for this," I said. This was exactly what I'd been hoping for, and I couldn't wait to get there.

The Youth Services Division of the Metro Police Department was in an old converted high school on Hayes Street in Northeast DC. Inside, it was exciting to walk through the bull pen where all the detectives had their desks. I wanted to know what every single one of them was working on, even though I was there for just one reason—to find out as much as I could about Gabe's case.

"Hey, Cross!" one guy said as we passed through. "How you hanging in there?"

"I'm hanging," Dad said.

"Keep the faith, man. We're behind you," he said.

"Thanks," Dad told him, but that was all he said. I knew that didn't mean the whole department was behind him, but at least a lot of these detectives were. Either way, I could tell Dad didn't want to talk about his upcoming trial. Maybe because I was there. Or maybe because we had other business to get to.

We kept moving and came to a little meeting room where Detective Sutter was already waiting for us. She got up and shook my hand when we walked in. "Thanks for coming, Ali," she said. "We have a lot to talk about."

I thought so, too, and even though I didn't mean to jump right in with a question, it was kind of like the question jumped out of me. They do that sometimes.

"Do you know if Gabe ran away?" I asked. "Or do you think maybe someone snatched him up?"

For me, that was the core of it right now. Five days missing was one thing if Gabe made himself disappear. But if someone had taken him and hadn't sent back any word in all that time about a ransom or anything? That was a whole lot closer to a worst-case scenario.

Detective Sutter didn't answer right away. She looked at Dad first, and he nodded at the detective to go ahead.

"Kidnapping is very rare," she said. "It's much more likely Gabe took off for whatever reasons of his own. We think he's in the general area based on his phone pinging off the cell towers, but we haven't been able to track it to a specific location because it's turned off most of the time. And we don't know if it's still in his possession. So he could be anywhere."

That was somewhere around a five on a scale of ten for reassurance, but I guess it was as much as she could tell me. Which of course made me wonder—what *wasn't* she telling? Not that I could ask that one.

Dad and I sat in metal chairs on one side of a big table, across from the detective. The only other thing in the room was a camera up in the corner, but I noticed the little red light wasn't on. I guess that meant they weren't recording. Probably because I wasn't a suspect.

"Let's start with the day Gabe disappeared," Detective Sutter said. "Did you notice anything out of the ordinary that afternoon? Anything unusual in the way Gabe was acting?"

"Not in a bad way," I said.

"What does that mean?"

"I mean, Gabe just kind of *is* unusual. My great-grandma says he marches to his own drummer, but I think he's just quiet. Or shy. Both, I guess. I always thought if Gabe had a superpower, it would be invisibility, if you know what I mean."

"Not really," Sutter told me. "Can you say some more about that?"

"Well..." I didn't really want to talk about Gabe

55

behind his back, but it was important to tell the truth. "It's like he spends a lot of energy just working on not being noticed. He doesn't even eat lunch with me and my friends at school."

"Where does he eat lunch?"

I shrugged because I didn't know. It had bothered me at first when we'd ask him to eat with us and he'd shake his head, but I figured after a while it wasn't anything against us. "That's kind of the point. He mostly keeps to himself. I think he's like some kind of genius, if you ask me. It's like his brain runs harder than anyone I know."

"Except maybe yours," Dad said, which was kind of embarrassing. I'd never call myself a genius. But at the same time, Gabe and I were kind of alike that way, always thinking hard about something or another. I'd see him in school sometimes, staring into space, and I could just tell he was working on some new invention, or idea, or whatever else. Only because I was the same way.

"Was I the last one to see him before he disappeared?" I asked.

"I'm not sure," Detective Sutter told me, and

then kept going. "So, you said he was supposed to meet you online that night. Where was that going to happen?"

"In *Outpost*," I said.

"Excuse me?"

Dad stepped in for that one. "It's a video game. Ali and his friends play it constantly."

Detective Sutter wrote a note in her file. "And he never showed up for the game?" she asked.

"Nope. And he hasn't been online since then, at least not at the same time as me. He hasn't answered any of my messages or texts, either," I said. "Do you know if his phone is still working?"

"We've submitted a subpoena to his carrier," she told me. "There should be some word soon. But if he took out the SIM card, or if someone destroyed it, then that's going to be a dead end."

I knew that much myself. Once you take the SIM card out of a phone, it stops pinging off cell towers, and then there's no way to track it. Gabe would have known it, too. He was plenty smart enough to make sure nobody was spying on him, if that's what he wanted.

"Why does it take so long to get that info—" I started to ask, but Detective Sutter cut me off right there.

"Ali?" she said. "I know you're eager to get as much information as you can, but I really need you to focus on *my* questions right now. Do you think you can do that for me?"

It was kind of embarrassing. Dad was looking at me like I'd forgotten the instructions he'd given me back at the restaurant, which I basically had. Obviously, I was going to help the investigation however I could. It was just hard keeping my own questions to myself.

After that, Detective Sutter asked if Gabe was having any problems at home (I didn't know), if he had a second phone (not that I knew about), and if he'd ever had a girlfriend or boyfriend (not even close).

She asked a bunch of questions about gaming, too, like what else Gabe played, when he was online, and what his screen name was.

I knew what she was getting at with the gaming stuff. Dad gave me the "online safety" lecture all the time, about how predators come after kids that way, and how easy it is to pose as someone else on the internet. I didn't know if Gabe was careful with that stuff, but I did know he basically lived for *Outpost*. He spent more time in that game than anyone I knew.

Finally, Detective Sutter closed her file and looked me right in the eye.

"I want you to know we're doing everything we can to find your friend," she said. "I mean it, Ali. This case is important to me."

I believed her, too. I know how seriously Dad takes his own job, but I also know that he doesn't get a win every time. That's just not how it works.

Meanwhile, the clock was ticking. Every day Gabe stayed missing, the trail was going to get a little colder. Maybe I wasn't going to get all the answers I was hoping for from Detective Sutter, but that didn't mean I was out of questions.

Just the opposite. I still had about a million of them. And as far as I was concerned, I was going to keep on looking for some answers of my own.

CHAPTER 9

AFTER DAD DROPPED me off at home and went back to work, I got busy. First, I went up to his office in the attic and pulled out one of the big bulletin boards he uses for his investigations. That's where he gathers everything together like puzzle pieces when he's launching a new case. And since he was stuck on desk duty until his trial, he wouldn't be needing those boards anytime soon.

I brought one down to my room and leaned it against the wall. Then I grabbed a map of Washington

DC from our kitchen junk drawer and tacked it onto the board. I stuck in two more thumbtacks, one for Washington Latin Middle School and one for Gabe's house on 17th Street. After that, I used a yellow highlighter to mark the way he usually walked home. I didn't know how far Gabe got that day before he disappeared, but if there was a crime scene, it was probably somewhere along that yellow line.

I knew what Dad would do with that part, too. He'd pull the footage from all the city traffic cameras along Gabe's route for the afternoon he disappeared. Detective Sutter had probably already done that herself, to see if she could tell how far Gabe got. But I hadn't—not yet. I wrote TRAFFIC CAMERAS on an index card, and tacked that up on the board, too.

Next, I jumped online to missing.dc.gov. That's where the police department listed all its missing persons cases. You can filter the page for juveniles, which is anyone under eighteen, and when I did that, it gave me thirty-one results. That meant thirty-one missing kids in DC. And right there at the top was the newest entry: Gabriel Qualls.

It was weirder than weird to see Gabe's school picture like that, with the words CRITICAL MISSING in a red bar above his head. They also had his description, where he was last seen, what he'd been wearing, and a phone number to call with any leads. The whole thing was a printable PDF, and I made two copies. One went on my board and the other went into my backpack, so I'd always have it with me.

After that, I just started brainstorming. I took some more index cards and filled them up with all the different things I wanted to know about—one idea for every card. Those went onto the board, too.

TRAFFIC CAMERAS
ANY WITNESSES?
CANVASSING THE NEIGHBORHOOD
SCHOOL
GABE'S PHONE WORKING?
HOSPITALS
SOCIAL MEDIA
MR. AND MRS. QUALLS
OUTPOST

When I stepped back and looked at everything I had, two things jumped out at me.

First, I texted Bree at work to ask about the traffic cameras. She was chief of detectives at MPD now. If anyone in our family could help with this, it would be her. Couldn't hurt to try, anyway.

ME: Hey Bree, I have a huge favor to ask. Any chance I could see the traffic cameras on E Street between Wash-Latin and 17th Street for December 21st, from 3:30pm to 5:00pm? It's about Gabe. Thanks if you can help!!!

The other thing that seemed worth looking into right away was Mr. and Mrs. Qualls. My guess was, they'd have at least some kind of information I could use, and maybe one or two things Detective Sutter hadn't told me, if I asked the right questions.

Also, now that I had it in my head to go talk to them, I didn't want to wait another second to make it happen. But first, I was going to need some kind of cover.

I'm not allowed to just "wander the streets of Washington," as Nana Mama likes to put it. But I am allowed to go alone to the store, or to school, or to some of my friends' houses during the day, depending on where they live.

So I made a quick plan. Then I put on my coat, grabbed my backpack, and headed downstairs.

"Where exactly are you off to?" Nana asked when I passed by the kitchen. She's in charge when Dad and Bree are at work.

"You want anything from the store?" I asked.

"Maybe just a little world peace," she said. That was always her answer.

"I'll see if they have any," I told her. And a second later, I was gone.

CHAPTER 10

BY THE TIME I ran to Gabe's block on 17th Street, I was too out of breath to be nervous about what I was doing.

Gabe's place was a two-story rowhouse. One of the windows was cracked with a piece of silver duct tape covering it, and there were ragged bedsheets hung up inside instead of curtains. The front door had those paper scraps from an old eviction notice that nobody had ever bothered to clean off. I'd always felt kind of sorry for Gabe every time we passed by there, and I could guess why he never wanted me coming in.

So I'd never even met his parents before, and didn't know much about his family at all.

When I knocked on the door, nobody answered for a long time. I could hear the TV volume up loud, so I knocked again, harder.

A second later, the door banged open. The white man who answered looked straight out, but then down at me, like he'd been expecting someone taller.

"What?" he said.

"Mr. Qualls?" I asked. I was a little surprised. Gabe had lighter skin than mine, but I didn't even know his dad was white. That's how clueless I was.

"Who are you?" he asked back.

"I'm Gabe's friend, Ali," I said.

"Oh, yeah. I've heard of you," he said. "The dirty cop's boy."

I don't know what I'd been expecting. My dad's always saying how people respond to trauma in all different ways, so I didn't want to jump to conclusions about Mr. Qualls. That's a rookie mistake for any detective. Maybe he was just mad about his kid being missing.

"I don't mean to bother you," I said. "I was just wondering if there was anything I could do to help out."

"Yeah. You could tell that father of yours to find my boy," he said. "How about that?"

"Actually, do you think I could take a quick look at Gabe's room?" I asked.

"Excuse me?"

I was losing my nerve fast, like water running down the drain. Mr. Qualls wasn't small like Gabe. Just the opposite. And I didn't know where the tattoos on his neck and arms came from, but I wasn't asking, either.

"I was just thinking, maybe he left something behind?" I said. "And maybe I could...I don't know...check it out, if that's okay?"

"I ain't got time for this," Mr. Qualls said with a dismissive wave of his hand. "Go home, kid. Let your daddy's people do their work."

"Maybe I could come back later—" I started to say, but that's as far as I got before the door closed in my face. And I definitely didn't have the nerve to knock again.

Now I was just standing there on the sidewalk, wondering what I was doing wrong. Between Dad, Detective Sutter, and Mr. Qualls, I'd basically struck out—one, two, three. Gabe deserved better than that. Maybe I just wasn't thinking about it the right way. Maybe I needed to stop trying to do this all on my own.

So I decided to do what Dad usually did at this phase of any investigation.

It was time to start pulling together my own team.

Chapter 11

When Bree got home from work, she had a surprise for me. It was a thumb drive with the traffic camera footage I'd been asking about.

"You can't keep this," she said. "We'll look at it together, but then I have to delete the files."

"Did you get this from Detective Sutter?" I asked.

"I did," she said. "It sounds like you impressed her with your questions."

"More like I bugged her with too many of them,"

I said. Mostly, though, I was glad to get my hands on this information. "Can we look at it now?"

"Sure can."

Bree opened her briefcase and took out the Toughbook laptop she used in the field for her own investigations. Once it was open, she navigated to an .avi file with a long name that was just a bunch of letters and numbers.

"I've got two of these for you," she said, and clicked the first one open. When the player started up, I saw a black and white image that was obviously from a camera mounted on a traffic light. Along the bottom of the screen, it said "E Street, 3700 block." That was maybe a block away from school.

For about fifteen seconds, I saw cars, buses, and random people going by on E Street. But then Gabe walked into the frame.

I practically lost my breath when I saw my friend. According to the date stamp, this was December twenty-first at 3:34 p.m., just a minute or two after he'd headed away from me outside of school.

"So that's the first clip," Bree said, while we watched Gabe cross out of the frame. Then she switched to another file and hit Play. This one was two blocks down and three minutes later, at the corner of E Street and 14th.

"There he is," she said. It was just a blurry image of Gabe with that same backpack of his, the one I'd seen him wearing outside of school that day.

"Hang on. What's in there?" I asked, and hit Pause. I put my finger on the screen over his back-pack. It looked pretty heavy.

"Why do you ask?" Bree said.

"Gabe never carried a bunch of books home like that," I told her. "Especially not for winter vaca-tion." I'd actually made a joke to him once, about the way that black and silver Spurs pack of his was always flopping around on his back, like all he ever brought to school was a bag full of air.

But not in the video. It was definitely weighed down with something that day. I hadn't noticed it either way when I last saw him, but it stuck out to me now. Like maybe he'd packed up a bunch of stuff to run away? "I'm just wondering what's so heavy in there. Can I take a screenshot?" I asked.

Bree shook her head. "Sorry, kiddo. I'm out on a

limb just by showing this to you. Try to take a mental snapshot if you can."

I'd already done that. It was something, anyway. Maybe a clue. And I'd definitely be letting Detective Sutter know about it. This qualified as unusual, if you asked me, and that's what she'd wanted me to try and remember.

Already, I was in front of my new bulletin board, looking at the yellow highlighter line on my map of DC, the one that showed Gabe's usual route home after school.

"So somewhere between that spot at 14th Street and 17th Street where he lives, he changed course," I said.

"Looks that way," Bree said. "But don't draw too many conclusions. Maybe he just had an errand to run."

"Well, he didn't go straight home, anyway," I said. "Not the way he usually walks. Otherwise, he would have kept going down E Street until 17th. But instead, he must have turned onto 15th or 16th. The question is, which direction? And why?" I looked at the map again, checking north and south of E Street. "It's too cold to be sleeping in Anacostia Park, but maybe he was trying to get across the river?"

Bree closed up the laptop and started putting it away. "Listen to you," she said. "You sound just like your dad."

She was looking at me the way Bree does sometimes. Like a proud mom, I guess you could say. I came back over and put my arms around her. She always smelled really good, too. Like vanilla ice cream or something. "Thanks for doing this," I said.

"I figured you could use a little boost," she told me. And she was right about that.

I still had endless questions about what was going through Gabe's head that day after school, but still, this was more like actual progress than anything else I'd gotten done so far. And I wasn't finished for the day yet, either.

Not even close.

CHAPTER 12

AFTER DINNER THAT night, I went straight to the TV in the basement to play *Outpost*. When I logged on to the server, I saw that Lowkey-Loki, Cagey-B, and Blackhawk were already online. Those were the screen names for Cedric and our other friends, Mateo and Ruby. The only one missing from our usual squad was Gabe—also known as QUB in the game. From his profile I could see he hadn't logged in since he went missing.

"Hey, I'm here," I said into my headset, once I'd connected to a party chat. "What's going on?"

"Yo," Cedric said. "Just waiting for you."

"You find anything out from your dad?" Ruby asked.

They all knew Gabe had disappeared, of course, but somehow we hadn't talked about it much. If we did, it would be like admitting he was really gone. But now I needed their help, so I caught them up on everything I'd done so far, including the meeting with Detective Sutter, my conversation with Mr. Qualls, and what I'd learned from the traffic camera videos.

"Dang, you've been busy," Ruby said.

"Well, yes and no," I said. "I still have a whole ton to do. I was actually hoping you guys would get in on this with me."

"In on what?" Cedric asked.

"My investigation," I said. I knew that Cedric, Ruby, and Mateo were only friends with Gabe because of me. They never hung out with him when I wasn't around, so I had to come at this kind of carefully.

"Your *investigation*?" Mateo said. "Oh, man. You are such a geek."

"Nah, he's just Alex Cross's kid," Cedric said. "It's in the blood."

In fact, they were both right. I knew it wasn't a real investigation. Obviously. But at the same time, what else was I going to call it?

"I was thinking we could start out by checking Gabe's base station," I said. "As long as we're in the game anyway."

"Yeah, all right. Let's do it," Ruby said, and we all joined a new game.

In *Outpost*, the playing area is one big island, but you can build your own home base wherever you want. It can be a watchtower, a house, a barracks, or whatever else you feel like coming up with. The more resources you pick up while you play, the more you can trade those in for building supplies, weapons, vehicles, or upgrades to your avatar. The whole point is to be as much of a good guy or bad guy as you want; build stuff if you feel like it; and try to survive for as long as possible.

I knew Gabe liked building stuff in *Outpost* at

least as much as he liked shooting stuff, so I was thinking his home base was probably going to be pretty sweet. And if I couldn't get a look at his actual room on 17th Street, maybe his virtual one in the game was the next best thing. Maybe I could find a clue about what he'd been up to before he disappeared.

So once we were ready to go, I cashed in five hundred units from my bank to requisition a four-seat all-terrain vehicle for Blackhawk, Lowkey-Loki, Cagey-B, and me.

My own screen name was Cassius Play. As in Cassius Clay, also known as Muhammad Ali, the greatest boxer who ever lived. He's my dad's idol, and that's who I'm named after.

So as soon as we were all on board, I put the pedal to the metal of that ATV and started driving toward the quadrant where I knew Gabe had built his place. Ruby (well, Blackhawk) rode shotgun, with Cedric (Lowkey-Loki) and Mateo (Cagey-B) in the back. The guys had swivel seats, so they could watch out for enemy fire and keep us covered along the way.

Sure enough, we hadn't gone far before I heard Cedric over my headset.

"Hold up. We've got some trouble here," he said. Another squad was coming up on us, probably hoping to snag that ATV for themselves.

"Behind you!" Ruby said, just before Mateo fired off a laser spray that took out most of the problem in one shot. I checked my rearview mirror and saw half a dozen avatars on the ground, receding into the distance while I kept us moving.

"Nice!" I said. I had to focus on driving, so defense was on them.

"Watch that sniper!" Cedric said.

"Got it," Ruby answered. On screen, Blackhawk fired two fast pulses up into the trees. A second later, some random alien creature dropped to the ground, flopping its blue tentacles for a second. But then it didn't move.

"That's right, son! Nobody messes with us!" Mateo said. His voice cracked at the end, and I didn't even try not to laugh.

"Who's the geek now?" I asked.

After that, I spent another two hundred units on some shields for the ATV so we wouldn't be bothered the rest of the way there. I still needed to talk some more about the Gabe stuff while we traveled.

"So listen," I said. "I want to start canvassing soon, in real life."

"Canvassing?" Cedric asked.

"It's what cops do on a case like this. You go out in the neighborhood where the missing person was last seen and start talking to people, looking for witnesses, and handing out flyers. That kind of thing."

"Dude, you live in a house full of detectives," Cedric said. "What do you need us for?"

That was about as complicated as a question got. I didn't know if Cedric and the others knew about Dad's trial, but I wasn't going to dig into that right now.

"Whatever," I said. "I'll do it myself if nobody wants to help."

"Nah, I'm on it," Cedric said.

I didn't mean to call him out like that, but I knew Cedric would be up for helping if I pushed just a little. He's also really big for his age—he kind of looks like Lebron, but without the beard—and it never hurts to have a little muscle on your side.

"Our parents are a no-fly zone for anything like that," Ruby said. "We can't be going around talking to strangers on the street."

"Speak for yourself," Mateo said. "I'll help."

"Oh, so you're going to go up against Daddy on this?" Ruby asked. "Yeah, I'm so sure."

Ruby and Mateo were brother and sister. They were also preacher's kids. Their dad, Reverend Sandoval, was from another big city—Buenos Aires in Argentina—and he was even stricter than my dad. They weren't allowed to go anywhere without an adult.

"There's still other stuff you could do," I said. "Actually, Ruby, I was thinking you could get all over social media with this."

Ruby had more than seven hundred followers on Instagram. I had like twelve, including my family members. Even Gabe had way more than me, but they were all gamers and *Outpost*-heads.

"I can do that," she said.

"Anyway, hold that thought," Mateo said, "because I think we're here. Check it out, straight ahead."

On the TV screen in front of me, I could see where some kind of building was just coming into sight through the woods. And since there was nothing else around, it seemed like we'd come to the right spot. Gabe really was a loner, in the real world as much as the virtual one. No wonder he'd built his place all the way out here.

As for whether our little side mission was going to be worth the effort, I guess we were about to find out.

CHAPTER 13

GABE'S PLACE WAS a simple bunker from the outside. It looked like a big corrugated steel half-cylinder lying on its side, with no windows and just one door that I could see.

"That's it?" I heard Ruby ask over my headset. "I mean, no offense to Gabe, but I thought he was some kind of genius with this stuff."

"Just wait. I'll bet he's got a sick underground compound in there," Mateo said.

"That'd be so Gabe," Cedric added. "Little dude is like, not much on the outside, but super deep on the inside."

I was thinking the same thing. My guess was he'd designed this base to look lame on purpose, so if anyone wandered into this quadrant and spotted it, they'd just keep moving.

Not us, though. We were already out of the ATV and spreading out to check the surrounding area. The bunker was on a cliff looking over the ocean, with Outpost's three moons hanging in the sky— one red, one orange, and one white. I did a quick lap around the building to check it from all sides, and jumped up on the roof, too. Sure enough, the only door was on the south side, where we'd started. By the time I got back around to it, Cedric's avatar was already trying to break in.

"Door's locked," he said, and didn't waste any time giving it a couple of full roundhouse kicks. Not that it did any good. The door looked like reinforced steel, and it didn't budge.

"Hang on. What's this?" Ruby asked. On my

screen, I saw her slide open a little panel embedded in the door itself. Inside that, there was a keypad. "Looks like some kind of combination lock."

The keypad was just letters, no numbers, with five spaces on the input screen.

"So the combination's some kind of five-letter word?" Cedric asked.

"Or maybe just a random sequence," Mateo said.

I went in close on the keyboard and punched in G-A-B-E-Q, just to try something. But when I hit Enter, all I got was a soft clunking sound. No surprise there. Gabe was too smart to make it that easy.

"Any other ideas?" I asked.

"Yeah, I got an idea," Cedric said. "Stand back."

On screen, Lowkey-Loki was already powering up his wrist cannon and taking aim at the door again.

"Wait!" I said, about half a second too late. He'd already fired off a white-hot blast at full power. His laser rebounded off that door and rippled right back at us, like some kind of sci-fi explosion. I heard a loud bang, and the whole screen went blue, right before it all faded out to black.

Just like that, I was back outside the game. Cassius Play was rotating on the welcome screen, with a damage report scrolling across the bottom. His energy reserves were down to 8 percent from whatever had just booted him to kingdom come.

"Ohhh, man! That was *harsh*!" Mateo said. "But also...awesome. How did he even set that up?"

"Does everyone need to regenerate?" I asked.

"I do," Ruby said.

"Yep," Cedric said. "My bad. Sorry about that."

"No worries," I said. "If anything, it just tells us that Gabe didn't want anyone in there. And you know what that means, right?"

"Yup," Mateo said. "Now I want to get into that place more than ever."

"Exactly," I answered.

It was just like they say, how still waters run deep. Gabe was like this quiet kid who only ever showed off when he was inside this game and hiding behind an avatar. In a weird way, it made sense. He may have been shy, and maybe even kind of weird, but that didn't mean he didn't have mad skills. In other words, Gabe Qualls was a stealth genius. I just hoped that wherever he was, all those skills might translate into the real world when he really needed them.

"I knew getting in there wouldn't be so easy," Ruby said.

"He must have set this all up at least a week ago," I said. "Gabe hasn't even logged in since he disappeared."

"Well, maybe," Mateo said. "That's the other thing, right? All we know for sure is that QUB hasn't logged in."

"Exactly," Ruby said. "He could use any screen name he wants in there. Any avatar, too. It doesn't have to be QUB."

"For all we know, we drove right by him," Mateo said.

"For all we *really* know, he could have been sitting inside that bunker watching us the whole time," Ruby said.

A chill went snaking down my spine. I hadn't even thought about that, but of course they were right. Just because I knew Gabe Qualls better than anyone else at school didn't mean I *really* knew him. Maybe nobody did.

And now, I was starting to wonder just how many secrets Gabe might have been sitting on, long before he ever disappeared.

CHAPTER 14

THE NEXT DAY, I went with Dad and Bree to Jannie's indoor track meet at the Johns Hopkins University Field House in Baltimore. Damon was already back at college, and Nana stayed home to rest. It was just the three of us representing for Team Cross in the stands.

The regular indoor season was on holiday break. This was an invitational with college scouts from Morehouse, Lincoln University, Penn State, and I don't even know where else. Jannie was running the 400 meter, her best event, so it was a huge opportunity for her and for Eastern High.

My sister and brother are definitely the jocks in our family. I'll run with Jannie sometimes, or shoot hoops with Damon, but I'm not exactly the athletic scholarship type. Bree says I'm a mental jock, and I'll take it.

So while we were waiting for Jannie's race to start, I kept working out my brain, thinking about all the Gabe stuff. I figured he never got a day off from being missing, so I wasn't going to take a day off from looking for him.

"Hey, Dad?" I asked. "Do you know anything about Mr. Qualls?"

"Gabe's father?"

"Yeah. Or his mom," I said.

"I've spoken with his mom a few times," Dad told me. "And I know his dad was out of the picture until September or so. I'm pretty sure he was incarcerated."

Gabe had never said a word about that.

"What was he in jail for?" I asked.

"I don't know," Dad said.

"Do you know if he's a person of interest in Gabe's case?" I asked. "Like a suspect, or whatever?"

"Ali." I could already hear that big red stop sign in Dad's voice. "You need to be careful about sticking your nose in where it doesn't belong. Got it?"

I wanted to say, "yeah, too late for that," but I couldn't admit I'd already gone over to Gabe's house. What I really wanted was for Dad to go there, too, but now wasn't the time to push it.

"Here we go!" Bree said. "Come on, Jannie! You got this!"

I looked over at the track and saw Jannie coming out of the tunnel with the other sprinters in her heat.

"She looks nervous," Dad said.

"She'll be great," Bree said.

Jannie had pulled the fourth lane for her starting position. That put her next to Claire Wilson from Anacostia High School. Claire was Jannie's number one rival. Her best time in the 400 was half a second better than Jannie's, which was actually a good thing. Jannie always worked a little harder when Claire was in the mix. Both of them were shaking out their feet now, rolling their heads, and eyeing the track ahead.

"On your marks!" came a voice over the loudspeaker, and everyone settled in for the start. Jannie didn't use blocks, but she leaned in, ready to take off.

"Get set," the voice said.

Then a starter pistol fired, and all eight runners took off flying.

"That was a hot start!" Bree said.

"She's gonna burn out!" I said.

"Pace yourself, Jannie!" Dad shouted.

Usually, Jannie saved her big kick for the last hundred meters, but she'd started this race running full-out from the get-go. I think those college scouts might have had something to do with that.

It was a staggered start, so everyone had to stick to their lanes for the first lap. That made it hard to know who was ahead until they came out of the second curve. Then everyone shifted to the inside. And right there at the front of the pack was Jannie. Her shoulders were down, her head was up, and her stride was long and even.

"That's some nice form!" Dad yelled.

"You got this!" Bree shouted.

But it wasn't over yet. On the next half lap, Claire picked up some steam and took over the lead. Another girl was coming up on Jannie fast, too. I saw Jannie check over her shoulder, which she never does.

"Focus, Jannie, *focus*!" Dad yelled. I think everyone in the field house was yelling now. I could feel the noise on my arms like goose bumps.

Jannie held on to second place through the next curve and into the last straightaway, with about a hundred yards to go. But she still hadn't caught up to Claire.

"She's doing great," Bree said. "Even if she snags second place, she might still..."

But then Bree stopped talking and grabbed Dad's arm instead. Because it looked like that big kick of Jannie's—the one we thought wasn't coming— had just *kicked* in. She was making Claire work for it now, and you could tell Claire knew it. Both of them were sprinting it out toward the finish.

"Come on, Jannie!"

"Dig! Dig! Dig!"

"Go, J.C.!"

With maybe thirty yards left, Jannie got right alongside Claire. Then she was up. Then back again.

"You've got this!" Dad boomed out.

Jannie leaned in at the line. So did Claire. It was too close to call on a visual, and I think every head in that place whipped over to look at the board for the final standings.

1. JCROSS 58.05

2. CWILSON 58.59

Everyone from Jannie's school went crazy in the stands. So did we. A bunch of people started chanting her name. I could see some of those college scouts scribbling in their notebooks, too.

So it was a pretty great day for the Cross family. I mean, yeah, Jannie can be a pain in the butt as my older sister. But when she's on the track, I'm *always* proud of her. I only wish I could run like that.

Other than with my brain, I mean.

CHAPTER 15

LATER THAT NIGHT, I was up in bed reading my new Spy School book, when the doorbell rang downstairs.

I sat up fast. The clock by my bed said 11:51.

Then the bell rang again. And again. And again.

What the heck was going on? It felt like Christmas Eve in reverse, with us inside the house and *someone* on the outside, trying to get in.

A second later, I was on my feet. When I opened the door to the hall, Bree and Dad were already there. Jannie was standing in her own doorway, and we were all looking at one another. The bell had stopped ringing, but that didn't mean we were in the clear.

"What was that?" Jannie asked.

"Stay here," Bree said. "I've got it."

Dad had his phone out, ready to call 911, but he waited with his hand on it, like a weapon at his side. Bree went down the stairs and stopped at the door to look through the glass. Then she opened it and stuck her head outside. I could see her looking up and down 5th Street.

"Anything?" Dad called to her.

"I don't think so," she said. But then, "Actually, hang on."

She bent over to pick something up from the stoop. For a couple of silent seconds, all I heard was my own breathing, a little faster than before.

When Bree closed the door and turned around again, she was holding a white plastic garbage bag. There was something heavy inside, poking at the plastic. Or maybe a bunch of stuff, I couldn't tell.

"What is it?" Dad asked.

Bree looked down into the bag, then up at all of us standing there. "It looks like we've been un-robbed."

"We've been *what?*" Dad asked.

She held up the bag, without showing us what was inside. "I think we've got Ali's stolen laptop here. Also, a few other things they took from our room. You're going to want to call this in, Alex."

Her voice sounded weird, like there was something she didn't want to say, but I was pretty sure I knew what that was. Besides my laptop, I was guessing, someone had just returned the two police weapons that had been stolen from Dad and Bree's room. I didn't think Jannie had ever found out about that part, so I didn't mention it.

To be honest, I was more excited about getting my laptop back, even if I wouldn't get to touch it that night. It was going to have to go in for fingerprinting, and maybe digital forensics, too. Still, this was really good news for Dad and Bree.

"Why would they just return a *few* things?" Nana said, coming into the downstairs hall from her room on the first floor. "How does that make sense?"

"Maybe they figured out this was a cop house," Bree said. "That's another whole layer of trouble if you get caught."

"Or maybe they sold some of it before they changed their minds," Jannie said.

"That, too," Bree said.

But now, I was wondering about a third possibility. What if I was right about Gabe all along? What if he'd been the one to break into our house in the first place?

Maybe he'd seen my name on that gift-wrapped laptop under the tree, so he'd know it was mine. Maybe this was just his way of saying he was sorry for what he'd done. Even if he had kept—and maybe sold—some of our other stuff.

As for the guns, maybe Bree was exactly right. Maybe Gabe got sketched out about being responsible for a couple of stolen police weapons, so he'd returned them along with the laptop. I mean, yeah, it would have been super disturbing for my friend to do anything like this, especially to me. The only reason I could imagine him targeting our place was because he'd been inside before, and maybe knew how to sneak in and out pretty easily. But still, breaking and entering just wasn't like Gabe. Or, at least, it wasn't like the Gabe I knew....

He'd have to be pretty desperate to try something like this, and it cut me up inside, just thinking about it.

Except then I realized something else. If Gabe was the one ringing our doorbell a minute ago, that meant he was still somewhere nearby. Maybe *very* nearby.

In which case, every second I stood there was another second I'd wasted.

Already, my feet were moving. I booked down the stairs, past Bree, and straight out the front door to the street.

"Ali!" she shouted, but there was no stopping me now.

The streetlamps on 5th Street threw a little light, but not much. Mostly it was dark, cold, and quiet out there.

"Gabe!" I yelled. "Gabe, are you here?" I was looking back and forth, out of my mind, not really seeing anything. "Gabe! Come back! It's okay—"

Then I felt Dad's hand on my shoulder.

"Take a breath," he told me. I thought he'd be mad, but it didn't sound like he was.

"But what if—"

"Just *stop*," Dad said. "Stop what you're doing and take a breath. Let your mind come into focus."

So I did what he said. I took a breath.

"And another," Dad said. "Slower this time. Take control of the situation."

I didn't know exactly what he meant, but by the time I'd taken another slow breath and let it out, I did feel different. More focused.

"Now," Dad said. "Look around. Take it in. If you were trying to get away from our house, which way would you go?"

I looked up and down 5th Street again, and thought about it. G Street was way down to the left, but Virginia Avenue was only a few houses away, to the right.

"That way," I said, pointing right.

"Why?" he asked.

"It's quicker to get out of sight," I said. "And if I knew the neighborhood, I'd be going for the underpass on 6th Street. Then I'd get to the other side of the highway and disappear as fast as I could."

"Okay. Good," Dad said. "Now you're thinking like a detective. Anything else?"

"Um..." I wasn't sure.

"Don't ever forget to look up," he said. "Not just left and right. Always think in three dimensions. That could mean a rooftop, or even up a tree. Believe me, it happens."

I looked up, but all I saw were empty trees and the tops of houses that seemed too high for anyone to reach that fast. Much less Gabe. I was just over five feet tall myself, and Gabe was smaller than me.

"I don't think anyone's up there," I said.

"Probably not," Dad said. "But this is about possibilities, got it? Don't rule anything out without a good reason."

I was listening to everything he said, but I was still scanning the block, too, just in case.

"So then, it's *possible* that was Gabe at the door," I said. "Right?"

Dad pulled me closer and started steering me back toward the house now.

"I'd say that's a mighty long shot, Ali. I'm sorry," he said. "But point taken. We can't rule it out entirely."

"Maybe Gabe wanted me to have my laptop back," I said.

"Maybe," Dad said.

"And maybe he felt bad about taking your police weapons, too," I said.

Dad stopped and looked at me for a long time. I'm almost positive he was about to ask how I knew about the guns, but then it was like he changed his mind.

"You really are in deep with this, aren't you?" he asked.

"For sure," I said, "but that's how I am with everything, right?"

Dad laughed at that, in the good way. "True," he said as we headed inside. "And I'll tell you what else. It's better to care too much than too little. Every single time."

ALEX CROSS

EVEN AFTER EVERYONE had gone back to bed that night, and the house had gone quiet again, Alex Cross's mind was as crowded as ever. Sleep was out of the question. There was too much to think about.

Once he'd resigned himself to staying up, he retreated to the back porch to play a little piano. Playing always helped him relax, and he worked his way through a little Gershwin, a little Chopin, a little *Secret Life of Plants*. He liked changing it up.

Eventually, thoughts about work drew him back

up to his office. He left the piano behind and parked himself at the computer upstairs, trading one keyboard for another.

The trial was coming up fast. There were meetings with the lawyers to be had, briefs to review, and conversations that still needed to happen with the kids. The press coverage was only going to get more intense when the actual trial got underway, and it was going to be impossible to shield the family from all of it. Life was most definitely going to get harder for everyone before it ever got easier.

Then, just after one thirty in the morning, a *ding* on Alex's phone signaled an incoming text. It was from Isaac Olayinka, the lead investigator on the Christmas Eve robberies.

OLAYINKA: Hey Alex, I know you're probably asleep, but I heard from the desk sergeant that you'd called in the return of those two stolen weapons. Excellent news!

Alex texted right back.

CROSS: I'm awake. Still working, but yeah.

CROSS: Happy to have those in hand again, for sure.

OLAYINKA: Can you tell me what time that happened?

ALEX: Just before midnight, why?

OLAYINKA: We've had another run of robberies in your neighborhood tonight. Three houses within a six-block radius. Same basic pattern.

Alex sat back and reread that last text. Three more houses? That was seven in all.

CROSS: And we're the only ones who had anything returned?

OLAYINKA: So far, yeah. Weird, right? And hey, I know you're on admin leave, so you didn't hear this from me, but we're at 406 4th Street, if you're curious. The homeowner's in Florida. We'll be covering this place all night.

Alex appreciated the heads-up more than Olayinka might have known. Being stuck with desk duty for the past six months had left him feeling like a benchwarmer in the playoffs. Here was a chance to get back into the game. Unofficially, of course.

CROSS: I'll be right there.

ALEX CROSS

FIVE MINUTES AFTER his text conversation with Detective Olayinka, Alex was showing his badge to a uniformed officer at the yellow tape line outside 406 4th Street, where the latest robbery investigation was underway.

"I'm looking for Olayinka?" he asked.

The officer pointed him through the front door and straight back toward the kitchen, where the lead detective was already motioning him over.

"Thanks for the heads-up," Alex said as they

shook hands. "I'll try to be quick. What have you got?"

"We're not even sure what was stolen yet," Olayinka said. "But there are a few obvious gaps. Home electronics, a little jewelry from the bedroom."

"Déjà vu," Alex said.

"It's all very similar to what we've already seen, with one small exception," Olayinka told him. "Emphasis on the 'small.'"

Now he pointed to a swinging dog flap built into the outside kitchen door. A heavy plastic panel, usually meant to slide up and down to close off the opening, had been punched out. Several blue plastic shards lay on the kitchen floor.

"That's the only indication of forced entry this time," Olayinka told him. "Best I can tell, someone less than a hundred pounds came in that way."

Alex knelt by the broken dog door and pushed his arm through the poly flap that was still in place. His adult-sized head and shoulders would never fit.

"It wouldn't be the first time I've seen something like this," Olayinka kept going. "Some scumbag uses a kid to get inside, and then cuts them in for a few bucks."

Alex's mind spun, lining up everything he already knew with everything he was just now learning. There was the robbery at his own place around the corner. The returned items from a few hours earlier. And most of all, the conversation he'd had with Ali in the street. Was it possible his little genius of a son had been onto something?

Possible, yes.

Maybe even likely.

"Hey, Isaac, do you know Wendy Sutter?" Alex asked.

"She's with Youth Services, right?"

"That's right. You might want to give her a call in the morning."

"Okay," Olayinka answered slowly. "Because...?"

"There's a missing kid she's looking for," Alex explained. "His name is Gabe Qualls, and don't quote me on this yet, but I'm starting to wonder if he might be one of the ones you're looking for, too."

CHAPTER 16

CEDRIC SAID HE'D meet me outside of Washington Latin at two the next day. I printed up a whole bunch of flyers with Gabe's picture and brought them with me. I also showed up early, just so I could put in a little thinking time first.

It was weird to stand there outside of school again. The last time I'd been in that same spot was the last time I'd talked to Gabe.

"So I'll see you online tonight," I'd said.

"Try and stop me," he'd said.

Those were the words that kept circling back into my head. "Try and stop me." It wasn't the kind of thing a person would say if they knew they were about to disappear. Maybe that meant Gabe hadn't run away on purpose. Maybe something even worse really had happened to him.

Or, I thought, maybe that was just Gabe, playing it off so I wouldn't suspect anything. Maybe he knew exactly what he was doing that day, down to the last word. There was still the question of what he had stuffed in that backpack of his, too. Maybe he'd filled it with provisions, so he'd be ready when it came time to disappear.

I just couldn't be sure about any of it. Every time I came up with a reason why it might be one thing, I'd come up with a reason why it might be the other. And it was driving me crazy.

"Yo!"

When Cedric came up on me from behind, I jumped. Which was embarrassing.

"Where you at?" he asked.

"About a million miles away," I said. "I was thinking about Gabe."

"Yeah, I figured."

I played along and gave a smile. "Anyway," I said, and handed him a stack of flyers. "Let's hit this block first and talk to as many people as we can. Then we can work down toward 14th Street if we have time."

"Sounds like a plan," Cedric said. He took one side of E Street and I took the other.

Dad always says street interviews are some of the hardest. It's about getting people to slow down and pay attention, which nobody ever wants to do. But when I saw someone I recognized, that seemed like a good place to jump in.

I didn't even know her name, but she worked behind the counter at the carryout near school. "Excuse me," I said. "Have you seen this kid anywhere?"

The lady looked at the flyer but didn't take it.

"No, honey. Sorry," she said. "Friend of yours?"

"Yeah."

"Well, good luck."

"Can you take this with you?" I asked, but she was already gone.

And it kind of went on like that. A lot of people just kept walking when I tried to talk to them. But some of them stopped, and a few took my flyer. One or two even knew about Gabe already.

So it was going okay, anyway. Not great, but at least I was getting the hang of it.

Right up until Kahlil Weyland decided to walk by.

Just for the record, I hate Kahlil Weyland. We've been in the same class all our lives, and it's like he was born thinking he was better than me. I didn't want to talk to him about Gabe, or anything at all, but I forced myself to do it.

"Cross?" he asked.

"Wassup?" I said. "You know Gabe Qualls is missing, right?"

Kahlil looked down at my flyer like I was trying to hand him a piece of garbage.

"I heard," he said. "And I care about that, why?"

That was typical, right there. Kahlil always acted like the world owed him something for nothing. And he's built like a middle-school version of Michael B. Jordan in *Black Panther,* so he's nobody you want to mess with if you don't have to.

"I'm just asking people if they've seen him around," I said. "Or maybe if they noticed anything on the afternoon he went missing. It was right after school on the Friday before break—"

"Listen to you, cop's boy," he said. Not like it was a good thing. Which was weird, because Kahlil and I were the same that way. His dad was a uniformed officer in the Sixth Ward.

"What's your problem, anyway?" I asked. I was getting mad, fast. I should have just let him keep walking.

"Don't play like you don't know," Kahlil said. He was stepping up to me now, too. "My pops has people coming down on him every single day, and you know why? 'Cause of dirty cops like your dad giving good ones like my dad a bad name."

"You don't know anything about that," I told him. I could feel my fingers making a fist around those flyers in my hand. What I really wanted was to knock that stupid smirk off Kahlil's face.

But Cedric was paying attention to us now, too. "We got a problem?" he asked.

"Your boy here does," Kahlil said. He may have

been bigger than me, but he wasn't as big as Cedric. Also, it was two against one now. I could feel him backing off already.

"Yeah, I'm pretty sure you were just leaving," Cedric said.

"Whatever," Kahlil said.

"That's what I thought," Cedric said. I was glad he was there, but more than that, I wished I could have gotten rid of Kahlil so easily myself.

"You're no detective, Cross," Kahlil said, walking away. "And your buddy Gabe's probably dead by now."

If Cedric hadn't grabbed me back, I would have been on him for real that time. But it was just as well. I wasn't out here to get into it with anyone. I had a job to do. And if a mouth breather like Kahlil Weyland was going to keep me from doing it, then I wasn't much of a detective to begin with. So I let it go—for now.

I had to get back to work.

CHAPTER 17

NEW YEAR'S EVE snuck up on me, but with Dad's trial hanging over us and Gabe still missing, it didn't feel like much of a new start. Still, we celebrated as best we could. Cedric came over for dinner after our canvassing, and then Ruby and Mateo showed up with their folks. The adults all had dessert and hung out upstairs while we did our thing in the basement.

Supposedly we were having one of our movie nights down there. I put on *Endgame* just to make it sound like that's what we were doing. But really, we were there to talk about the Gabe stuff. It was like a shift change at the police department, where everyone reports out on what they know about an open case.

I started by telling the others how I'd gotten my laptop back, and how even Dad couldn't rule out the possibility that Gabe had been the one ringing our doorbell that night.

"You're saying Gabe broke into your house on Christmas Eve?" Ruby asked.

"I'm saying it's a possibility," I told her.

"Just so he could turn around and give you back your laptop?"

"Yeah, that doesn't make any sense," Mateo said.

"What about any of this makes sense?" I said. "Maybe we're just not asking the right questions yet."

"Like what kind of questions?" Cedric asked.

"Well, if we knew that, we'd be asking them," I said.

Cedric doesn't always pay attention all the time, but I wasn't going to be giving him a hard time about it here. He'd just spent the whole day out on the street with me, not to mention saving my bacon with Kahlil Weyland.

"So what else have we got?" I asked, and Mateo picked it up from there.

"I called all the hospitals on that list you sent me," he said. "None of them have a patient named Gabriel Qualls, or Gabe, or initial G."

"Thanks for checking, anyway," I told him.

"Well, hang on. Here's the other thing I was thinking," Mateo said. "What if Gabe's in the hospital but he doesn't know who he is?"

"Like amnesia or something?" Ruby asked.

Mateo shrugged. "What if he got knocked upside his head somehow, and he's walking around like one of those whaddya-callits? A Jack Doe."

"John Doe," Ruby said.

"Whatever," Mateo said.

"Amnesia?" Cedric was practically rolling on the floor by now. "Get serious, bro. This ain't a TV show."

"I'm just saying, you never know," Mateo answered.

116

"I know *you* watch too many movies," Cedric said.

That was true, too, for all of us. We were always down for anything Marvel, or DC in a pinch, or especially anything scary. The scarier the better, like *Get Out*, or *It*, or the Cloverfield movies, even though we weren't technically allowed to watch R-rated stuff. Nana always said those kinds of movies fed my imagination, and not in the good way. Maybe she was right, but I loved them all the same.

Meanwhile, this conversation wasn't supposed to be about movies. This was about Gabe, and I needed everyone to stay focused. I turned to Ruby next.

"Where are we at with social media?" I asked, since that was her department now.

"Nothing new on Gabe's Instagram," she said. "The last thing he posted was from the day before he disappeared, and that was a picture of some suspension bridge he built in *Outpost.*"

"*Everything* he posts is from *Outpost*," Cedric said.

If you ever wanted to know how Gabe's mind worked, all you had to do was look at his Instagram. It was full of crazy stuff he'd designed inside the game. There were vehicles, weapons, different kinds of body armor, and even temporary shelters you could fold up and take with you. Sometimes it seemed like Gabe must have spent more time in *Outpost* than he did in the real world.

"The one thing he never posted was a picture of his bunker," Ruby said.

"Probably because he didn't want anyone knowing about it," I said. "That's like his private spot."

"And you never figured out the combination lock on that door?" Mateo asked.

I shook my head. "Still working on it."

"Anyway," Ruby went on, "I've been getting some traction on my own Insta, with that MISSING flyer. And we're up to twenty-three shares on the Facebook page I set up, too. That's not bad, but we can kick it way up once we're back in school."

"Maybe we won't have to," Cedric said. "I mean, maybe Gabe'll be back by then. How long has it been, anyway?"

I didn't have to think about that one. I knew exactly how long it had been. "Ten days," I said. "And four hours, if anyone's counting."

Nobody said anything to that. It just kind of sunk in for a minute. They probably didn't know what I knew—that the chances of solving a missing persons case goes way down after three days because the clues dry up. And here we were at *ten*.

Ten days. I wondered where Gabe was right now. Or how cold he might be. Or how hungry. Or maybe even hurt.

Then Mateo spoke up again. "If this was some rich white boy, you know they would have found him by now," he said. "Or like that missing kid on *Stranger Things*—"

"Will Byers," I said. I loved that show. So did Gabe. I think he watched each season three times all the way through.

"Yeah, Will Byers from Hawkins, Indiana," Mateo said. "Kid goes missing and everyone acts like the world is ending."

"Again...*not* a TV show," Cedric said, and we all cracked up at that. Maybe we weren't supposed to be laughing, but sometimes you have to.

"Well, whatever," Mateo said. "The point is, Gabe's from Southeast DC, he's poor, and he's black, which is enough for nobody to care. Gabe's got no headlines on the news, no search parties, no nothing."

"I hear that," Ruby said. "But you know what he does have?"

"What?" I asked. I really wanted to know.

"*Us,*" Ruby said.

I was glad to hear them talking like this. Before Gabe disappeared, I'm not really sure they thought about him that much. But now it was like the longer they worked on this investigation, the more they really cared. And the more I felt like we had a real live team of our own, tracking him down.

"We're kind of like Easy Rawlins and his WRENS-L Agency," I said.

"Who's Easy Rawlins?"

"A character in a book," I said. "A black detective."

"Like your dad," Ruby said.

"Sort of," I said, but really I meant like me. Didn't say so, though.

"All right, then," Ruby said. "If we're going to do this, let's really do it."

"We got this, you guys," Cedric said.

"Hundred percent," I said. I really did have some

awesome friends. And now, more than ever, I was thinking, so did Gabe.

Ruby had her hand out and I put mine on top of hers. Then Cedric and Mateo piled on.

"For Gabe," I said.

And they all said it, too.

"For Gabe."

CHAPTER 18

RUBY WAS RIGHT about getting back to school. In fact, that Wednesday morning everything kicked in way more than I'd even been hoping.

When I got to Washington Latin, I went to advisory like normal. But during morning announcements, they said there was going to be an all-school assembly just before first period. And it was all about Gabe's case.

I seriously didn't see that coming. It was starting

to sound like a lot of people had noticed what was going on, after all.

Once we were all packed into the auditorium, our principal, Mr. Garmon, put Gabe's MISSING flyer up on the big screen, fifteen feet high where nobody could miss it. Then he started talking about how Gabe had last been seen outside of Wash-Latin, and about what people could do to help.

"This is a chance for us to pull together as a school community for the greater good," Mr. Garmon told everyone. "If you know anything about Gabe's disappearance, or even think you *might* know something, I want you to talk to an adult about it."

I kept looking around the auditorium. There were about three hundred and fifty kids in our school. Someone had to have seen *something* that day, didn't they? And even if not, I was glad people were paying attention.

"If prayer is your thing, then by all means pray for our brother Gabe," Mr. Garmon went on. "And if any of you need to speak with a counselor, Mrs. Noble and Mr. Villagrossa are here for you."

"Sounds like Gabe is the one who needs a counselor," someone muttered a few rows behind me. And not just *someone*. Kahlil Weyland. I'd recognize that voice anywhere. He and his idiot friends were being a bunch of dipsticks about the whole thing. As usual.

I kept cool, though. Ruby was raising her hand to say something now and I didn't want to take away from whatever she was about to do.

"Hey, everyone," Ruby said after Mr. G gave her the mike. "Just so you know, we have a Facebook page set up for Gabe. If anyone has questions or information, you can post them there. And we have a hashtag now, too, which is #FindGabeQualls, all as one word—"

"More like hashtag, #wheresthebody?" Kahlil said. And this time, my mouth went off before I could stop it.

"Shut up, Kahlil!" I said. I stood up and turned around to face him. "You know so much about this, why don't you tell us what happened? Huh? Go ahead, 'cause I sure would like to know."

That pretty much brought everything to a dead

stop. Kahlil just stared back at me like he was Mister Innocent, and Mrs. Rutkowsky started lecturing me about borrowing trouble at a time like this.

I felt stupid for losing my cool, especially when I wanted everyone listening to the assembly. So I just turned around and pretended Kahlil didn't exist. He wasn't worth the trouble. I told myself I wasn't going to mess with him at all anymore. No matter what.

And I didn't.

For all of about ten minutes.

CHAPTER 19

I **WASN'T LOOKING** for trouble that morning. I really wasn't. But sometimes trouble comes looking for you.

After the assembly, I was standing in the hall talking to some people about Gabe and minding my own business, when I heard someone call out my name.

"Cross! Yo, Cross! When's your dad's trial?"

I looked over, and it wasn't Kahlil this time, but close enough. It was Darius Riggs, who was basically Kahlil's lapdog. That is, if lapdogs wore size ten Jordans and XL Wizards jerseys to school. In fact, I could see Kahlil hanging back by the trophy case, grinning my way like this was some kind of game for him.

Meanwhile, Darius was still jabbering.

"You think that old guy your dad pushed down the steps is gonna die?" he asked. " 'Cause that's like a murder charge then, right?"

If this were a movie, I would have pulled out my secret X-Men powers just then and thrown Darius straight across the room with a flick of my mind. I wish. But I doubted Darius even knew what he was talking about, anyway. He was just saying what Kahlil told him to.

"Get a life, man," I said, and went back to talking to the kids I'd already been talking to. But then Kahlil decided to jump in on it, after all.

"That's what your pops is gonna get after his trial," Kahlil told me. "*Life*. As in, no parole."

It was like someone had flipped a switch in my brain. I turned back around so fast, Darius actually flinched. But it wasn't the lapdog I was coming for. Nope. It was the fool behind him, holding the leash.

I didn't have a plan. I didn't think about it at all. I just came straight at Kahlil and popped him in the

face with a hard right jab. And I guess those boxing lessons Dad liked to give me all the time must
have paid off, because blood shot out both sides of
Kahlil's nose. All down his front, too.

Now Kahlil's shirt looked like a crime scene, and
his eyes were bugged open wide. I don't know which
one of us was more surprised. All I know is that I
didn't move fast enough when Kahlil took the next
swing. I didn't even know he was left-handed until
his fist connected with my cheekbone, just under
the right eye.

I flew back. Next thing I knew, I was flat on the
floor of the hallway. My head was swimming, everything was blurry, and I could hear people starting
to yell.

"Fight, fight, fight..."

"Get him, Kahlil!"

"Stop it!"

Kahlil came for me again and pulled me up by
the front of my shirt. I thought for sure he was going
to knock me right out, but it didn't get that far. Mr.
Garmon was already in the mix, pulling Kahlil off
and getting me back on my feet. He was yelling,

too, louder than anyone else. Garmon could go full-on drill sergeant when he wanted to.

"Enough! What do you boys think you're doing?" he hollered.

"He started it!" I said.

"Didn't look that way to me," Garmon said.

"If I'd started it, you wouldn't be standing," Kahlil said.

"I'm standing," I told him. "What are you going to do about it?"

"Keep talking," he said, pointing a finger in my face. "This isn't over."

Then I called him a whole bunch of names, the kind that can get you a detention just for using *one* of them in school. But I couldn't help it.

"Who you think you are, Kahlil?" I kept going. "You're a nobody! And you want to know why? 'Cause you don't even try to pick on anyone your own size!"

Kahlil was shouting back, but I wasn't hearing it. The words were pouring out of me just like the blood pouring out of his busted nose. And I would have said a whole lot more—and maybe worse, too—if Mr. Garmon hadn't put a stop to it.

"That's it!" Garmon shouted. "Both of you, not another word!" He had me by the arm now and Mrs. Noble was there, too, keeping Kahlil back. Kahlil wasn't even trying to come for me anymore. He was just holding his sleeve up to his nose and killing me with his eyes instead. I think we both knew it was over.

A second later, Garmon started marching me off toward his office while Mrs. Noble took Kahlil in some other direction.

"I'm disappointed in you, Ali," Garmon said. "Today, of all days, when we just got done coming together for Gabe. And I'm surprised, too. I wouldn't have expected this from you...."

There was more, but I only kind of heard him. The right side of my face felt like it was on fire, and I didn't need any special powers to know that I had a black eye in my future.

Not to mention everything else headed my way now. Because the fact was, I'd just bought myself a whole new mountain of trouble that I couldn't afford.

ΛLEX CROSS

ALEX KNEW THERE had been a fight. Something between his son and another boy. He knew Ali was in one piece, but nobody had told him about the black eye. It was the first thing he noticed when he stepped into the main office at Washington Latin Middle School.

There was Ali in the waiting chairs, looking miserable and already red around the eye socket. In time, it would turn purple, and then yellow, Alex knew. He'd had his own share of periorbital hematomas.

Still, nobody likes to see their own kid in pain. Alex's stomach clenched at the sight of it.

"What happened?" he asked.

"I didn't know he was lefthanded," Ali said, like that was the question. After all those father and son boxing lessons in the basement, it seemed maybe Ali had learned a little too much about offense and not enough about defense. Word was that he'd given the other kid a bloody nose.

"Dr. Cross? Good morning."

Alex looked up to see the school principal, Geoff Garmon, smiling politely and motioning him over. Garmon crooked a finger at Ali to come as well. "Let's go, Ali. You, too."

Inside the principal's office, a few more things came clear. Garmon reported that Ali had taken the first swing, and Ali didn't try to deny it. That part was even more surprising than the brawl itself. Ali had been in his share of scuffles before, but he had never been one to pick on other kids, much less start a fight.

Then again, Alex knew, it hadn't exactly been smooth sailing for Ali lately. Between his friend's disappearance and his old man's upcoming trial, Ali was a walking pressure cooker these days. All that stress had to come out somewhere. But it didn't mean Alex could let him off the hook, either.

"You have anything to say for yourself?" he asked Ali.

"Sorry." Ali mumbled it out with his eyes down.

"I think we can do better than that," Alex said, and waited for Ali to look up.

"I'm sorry, Mr. Garmon," Ali tried again.

"In any case," Garmon continued, "we have a zero-tolerance policy on fighting at Wash-Latin, and it comes with an automatic four-day off-campus suspension."

At that, Ali's jaw dropped. Suspension was a big leap from the occasional detention he'd received, and he glanced at Alex as if he were expecting dear old dad to run some kind of interference on this. Which wasn't going to happen.

"I have no doubt Kahlil was getting under your skin," Mr. Garmon said. "But this kind of response is unacceptable, and you know that, Ali. You know it very well. I hope we can look forward to a more constructive attitude from you when you come back to school next Wednesday."

"Yes, sir," Ali said, eyes down again.

"Does that seem unfair to you?" Alex asked.

Ali only shook his head, pressing his lips together like he was working overtime to keep the words inside. Clearly he wasn't going to try and fight this suspension, but he was still plenty mad.

Which was fine. Ali didn't have to like his punishment. He just had to take it.

ALEX CROSS

"WHAT WERE YOU thinking?" Alex asked as they walked to the car. "For real, son. How did this happen?"

"Kahlil was talking about you," Ali said. Now that they were out of the office and on the street, he'd loosened up. Maybe it was something he didn't want to talk about in front of Mr. Garmon. "You should have heard what he was saying."

"Yeah, well, Kahlil can take a number," Alex

answered. "You know how many people are talking trash about me these days?"

"I know, but—"

"And are you planning on throwing a punch at every single one of them?" Alex asked.

Ali had no answer for that one, other than letting out a deep sigh. He really was carrying a heavy load these days.

"I appreciate you having my back. I mean that," Alex went on, with a hand on his son's shoulder. "And if someone takes a swing at you, that's one thing. But I didn't teach you to box so you could go around starting fights and handing out bloody noses."

"Just because I hit him first doesn't mean I started it," Ali said then. "He was the one coming at me with his talk about Gabe and about you, even though he should know better. His dad's a cop, too, you know!"

"Who's his dad?"

Ali shrugged. "Officer Weyland, I guess. He's a patrol officer in the Sixth Ward."

The name wasn't familiar to Alex, but it would

be soon enough. He'd be giving Mr. Weyland a call that evening.

"In any case, you won't be going anywhere for the next four days," Alex said. "No friends, no TV, and no PlayStation, either."

"*No PlayStation?*" Ali blurted out. That seemed to get the biggest rise of all.

"You heard me," Alex said. "And if you can't get your head around that, then it tells me you're not taking this seriously enough. Should I go on?"

"No, sir," Ali said. The kid was too smart to push it any further.

In fact, there was no more conversation at all until they were in the car and halfway home. Once they'd passed through the busy intersection of Pennsylvania, 11th, and E Streets, Ali spoke up again.

"Dad?" he asked. "If Mr. Yang dies in the hospital, are you going to be charged with murder?"

His voice had gotten small. It was heartbreaking to hear. Ali really was afraid. And for that matter, so was Alex.

"I hope not," he answered honestly. "But how about we cross that bridge if or when we come to it?"

"Yeah, okay," Ali said. And then, "Dad?"

"Yeah?"

"Well...I know what you just said, but if Mr. Yang dies...does that mean you *did* kill him? Technically, anyway?"

"Let me put it this way," Alex answered. "I didn't push Mr. Yang down those stairs. I know you know that, but it's also true that there were no witnesses, and some people are going to believe what they want to believe, regardless."

"Like Kahlil," Ali mumbled.

"That's right," Alex said. "Probably some other kids at your school, too. There are plenty of great cops out there, but also some number of bad ones, and too many of them have been found innocent in court when they shouldn't have been. It can be confusing with all this coverage in the news."

"But you're one of the good ones," Ali said. "Right?"

"I like to think so," Alex said. "But listen, son. I don't want you worrying too much about this trial. We're going to work through it. Together. That's a promise."

There was so much more Alex wanted to say. Ali really could have used some good news that morning, if not about the trial, then about the other thousand-pound weight on his shoulders—the Gabe Qualls case.

But it was too early to let Ali know that his own theory about Gabe's involvement in the house robbery was still on the table. It was just an idea at this point. There was no sense getting Ali's hopes up too soon. It made more sense to wait until Detective Sutter from Youth Services got a chance to connect with Detective Olayinka. Then maybe Alex could bring Ali into the loop a bit more.

But not today. Not yet. For the time being, it was all just bad news on top of bad news.

What a mess.

CHAPTER 20

FOR THE REST of the ride home, I kept my mouth closed. Just like my right eye, which had swollen shut. It wasn't that much of a fight, but I felt like my skull had gotten a beatdown from the Hulk.

Honestly, I had that feeling about my life in general. While Jannie and Damon were getting all kinds of shine for running track and playing ball, I was the one dragging Dad down to school in the middle of the day to clean up some mess I'd made.

It was like everything was spinning out of control all at once. Not just for me, but for Dad, too.

So what was the difference, anyway, between an accident and an assault by a police officer, if no one believed him? And why wasn't anyone giving me clear answers about that? I knew Dad didn't assault Mr. Yang, so how could any of this turn into a murder charge? And what would happen if it did?

I couldn't think about it too much, either, because I didn't want to cry in front of Dad. He always told me it was okay to cry, but that didn't mean it felt good to do it.

Mostly, I just wanted to get this trial over with.

And I wanted Dad to be found innocent of all charges.

And for Mr. Yang to pull through.

And for Gabe to be found. Hopefully soon.

I also wished I could take back the whole thing with Kahlil. I mean, I wasn't sorry about the bloody nose I gave him. If you ask me, he got exactly what he deserved. But that fight had also gotten me stuck inside my house for the next four days, just when the Gabe stuff was starting to heat up. And just when I needed to be out there working on it more than ever before.

Oh, man. What a mess.

ALEX CROSS

ALEX WAITED UNTIL after dinner that night to call Victor Weyland. Even then, he wasn't looking forward to it. From the sound of things, this kid Kahlil was no angel, but there was no escaping the fact that Ali had drawn first blood. Still, Alex thought, maybe he could play the cop card with Officer Weyland, just to establish some common ground between them. It was worth a try, anyway.

Alex put himself in his office and out of earshot of the family before he picked up his phone. Then he dialed the number he'd gotten off of MPD's central directory.

"Hello?" a voice answered on the second ring.

"Hi, Officer Weyland?"

"Speaking."

"My name's Alex Cross. I'm Ali's dad, and—"

"I know who you are," Weyland answered, followed by a long silence.

Still, Alex pushed on. "I wanted to touch base with you about what happened at school today. I'm hoping we can get these two boys together for a handshake. Maybe also let them talk things through—"

"Excuse me, Detective Cross, but I'm going to stop you right there," Weyland told him. "You're kidding me with all this, right?"

Alex clenched his jaw. "Why would I be kidding about anything right now?" he asked, trying not to sound as annoyed as he felt. This was supposed to be his thing. Usually, Alex could talk to anyone.

But Weyland wasn't having it. "Let's just say the optics on this speak for themselves," he answered.

"And what's that supposed to mean?" Alex asked.

"Violent cop, violent kid," Weyland said. "You don't really need me to do the math, do you?"

Alex turned away from the phone, long enough to check his own temper. Up to now, he'd gotten nothing but support from the Fraternal Order of Police, including his union reps and his fellow officers. He knew there were cops out there who saw him as one of the bad apples, but he hadn't been expecting to confront it in person. Much less over a middle school fight.

"I assume you're talking about the Walter Yang case and my trial," Alex said, as calmly as he could. "Have you even read the report? Or do you just assume you know what happened?"

"I'm not going to get into it with you," Weyland shot back. "I already have enough to deal with out there, thanks to cops like you. Just keep your boy away from mine unless you want another lawsuit on your hands. And don't call this number again."

Unbelievable. It was maddening, but there was nothing Alex could do for it. Even if he wanted to continue the conversation, Victor Weyland had already hung up.

So much for finding common ground.

CHAPTER 21

AT LEAST I didn't have to apologize to Kahlil after our fight. I totally thought Dad was going to make me do that, but he never even brought it up. You *know* I never did.

He was serious about me being grounded, though. There was no going anywhere, no TV, no PS4—no fooling. When he and Bree went to work the next morning, I was on suspension at home with Nana. The only choice I had was whether I wanted to do my schoolwork at the kitchen table or the dining room table.

I took the dining room since Nana spent way more time in the kitchen. No offense to Nana Mama. It was more about trying to catch some time alone so I could work on the Gabe stuff. As much as that was possible without leaving the house, anyway. It was weird, like Dad and I had the same problem. We both wanted to be out there doing our thing, and we were both stuck on desk duty.

So I did what I could. While Nana thought I was working on a book report about *Brown Girl Dreaming* for my English class, I was also checking social media. And when I was supposedly doing some pre-algebra homework, I was actually googling for other missing kid cases in Southeast DC. I wanted to see if there might be any kind of pattern going on, but there wasn't, as far as I could tell.

In between all of that, I was also grabbing time whenever I could to text with Ruby, Mateo, and Cedric. It sounded like things were starting to hop on their end. Ruby and Mateo's dad was organizing a vigil at his church for Tuesday, and Cedric was handing out flyers before and after school. The social media numbers were going up and up, too.

RUBY: This is really taking off. You should be proud of yourself for getting it started.

ME: Thanks. I would have felt prouder if I'd been actually getting something done instead of just wishing and worrying about it at home. Still, Ruby was turning out to be a pretty awesome second in command.

The other thing I kept doing was sending texts to Gabe, at least a couple times a day. I didn't know if he was reading them, but it was as close to talking to him as I was going to get. I wanted him to know I was there, like a lighthouse sending out beacon after beacon, text after text. In a way, it didn't even matter what I wrote. I just wanted to keep that light on, in case Gabe ever needed it to help him find his way back home again.

ME: What's up? Did you know you have your own Facebook group now? And a hashtag, too. #FindGabeQualls

ME: You there? It's been fourteen days since you disappeared. I know maybe you can't talk, even if you are getting these messages. But I just wanted to say hey.

ME: Guess who got suspended from school? That would be me. I got in a fight with Kahlil W and survived, if you can believe that.

ME: Hey. Just saying hi.

ME: Please just answer me once if you're okay. I need to know.

ME: Hello?

ME: Anyone there?

ME: Please?

CHAPTER 22

I **WOKE UP** thinking about Gabe every day now. Went to sleep thinking about him, too. Every hour that went by was another hour where I felt like I should have gotten more done. It was like an ache in my brain. And in my heart, too. I couldn't focus on anything else.

Not even on the room around me sometimes.

"That doesn't look like social studies to me," Nana said, coming into the dining room, where

I was on day two of my at-home prison sentence. "What are you doing there, young man?"

I looked up from my texting to see Nana standing in the door from the kitchen. She'd already seen my phone and had her hand out to take it away. I didn't have much choice, so I gave it over.

"I was working on the Gabe stuff," I said. Confessed. Whatever.

I thought I was about to get a Nana-sized lecture, but instead, she just sat down and looked me in the eye. In a nice way.

"And how are we doing on that front?" she asked. "I imagine it's all very hard on you."

"I'm okay," I said. "I just can't stop thinking about it."

"Oh, I know," Nana Mama said. "I see it in you every day. The constant thinking, thinking, thinking. It's the price you pay for that fast running brain of yours."

"I just wish there was more I could do about it," I said. "To be honest, I feel like I let Gabe down by getting grounded. While I'm stuck here at home, he could be out there hurt, or hungry, or scared, or in a hundred different kinds of trouble—"

Nana cut me off. "That's the blessing and the curse of a mind like yours," she said. "An active imagination is a wonderful thing. But it can also be a burden, if you focus too much on the dark side of the street."

"It just all seems kind of impossible," I admitted. "I mean, I want to help, but how am I supposed to find Gabe if the police can't?"

"Impossible, huh?" Nana Mama sat back and eyeballed me, like she wasn't buying what I was selling. "Is that how all those detectives you admire so much get it done? Mr. Holmes? Monsieur Poirot? Olivia Benson? How far do you think any of them would have gotten if they worried too much about what was and wasn't *possible*?"

This is the thing with Nana. I knew she was right. I just didn't know how to take what she was saying and put it into action.

"Here's another name for you," Nana went on. "Do you know who James Baldwin is?"

"I'm not sure," I said. I knew he was somebody famous, but that was it.

"James Baldwin was a great American writer, poet, and thinker," Nana Mama told me. "And it was he who called black history a 'perpetual testimony to the achievement of the impossible.'"

I had to say that one out loud to really get it. "'A perpetual testimony to the achievement of the impossible.'"

Nana explained some more. "The life I get to live today would have been impossible for my great-grandmother, or even for my mother," she said. "And the things you can do now, as a young black man in this country, the things you can achieve? It all would have been impossible for me when I was your age. But it takes some faith, so don't ever let this notion of what's not possible stop you from trying. Anything is possible, Ali. And I mean that."

I saw what she was doing. She was telling me not to sell myself short. And I guess she'd know. She came up from nothing in North Carolina, and here she was, being a total boss in a house with two of Washington DC's baddest cops. Not too shabby.

"You're saying I can find Gabe if I set my mind to it," I said. "Is that it?"

Nana shook her head. "I don't know if you can," she said. "But there's one way to find out." Then she slid the phone back across the table to me. "No idle shenanigans, no chitchat with your friends. But if you want to work on your investigation, I'd call that a worthy bit of homework, after all."

"Thank you, Nana," I said.

"Don't thank me. Just do good work," she said. "And that includes all of your regular assignments for school, too. This isn't a free pass I'm giving you. It's *more* responsibility, not less. You got that?"

And of course I gave the only possible answer.

"Yes, ma'am," I said.

So maybe Nana Mama is kind of old school, or a lot old school, but I'll tell you what else: she's also one of the best, smartest, and, yes, coolest people I know.

No question.

CHAPTER 23

THE GOOD NEWS—part one—was that I got my laptop back from the police lab the next day. They'd dusted it for fingerprints, and I'm not even sure what else, but Dad brought it home for good that night.

And no, he told me, Gabe didn't have any fingerprints on record, so they couldn't check that. But I liked that he knew I was going to ask. It meant I was thinking about it like a real detective.

The other good news was that Damon's college

team, the Davidson Wildcats, were playing the Wake Forest Deacons that night, and the game was going to be on ESPN2.

I'd seen Damon play a million times, but never on TV. Nobody in the family had. And now he was playing for the same college team that Steph Curry had put on the map. It was like a national holiday at our house. Dad was even lifting my "no television" rule just long enough for me to get to see it.

I don't think our living room had ever been stuffed with so many people. Sampson and his wife, Billie, were there with their kids. We also had Dad's cousin Tia and her boyfriend, and Jannie's best friend Shaniece, who'd had a crush on Damon since forever. Nana had two friends from church, along with Father Bernadin, and a whole bunch of Dad and Bree's cop buddies were there from MPD, too. I wasn't allowed to have any of my own friends, since I was still grounded. But at least I got to watch the game.

Once everyone was there, I took a spot on the floor near the back of the room. That was for a couple of reasons. I was tired of everyone staring at my black eye and asking questions I didn't want to answer. Also, it was easier to sit back there and work on my laptop during the commercials if people weren't looking at me all the time. Now that I had my computer back, I wanted to load all my Gabe notes onto the hard drive so I could have it with me wherever I went.

"Let's go, Davidson!" Nana called out from the couch. She was all set up with her new app, so she could use her phone to track every move Damon's team made, down to the last block, shot, and assist. Anyone who thinks they know more about college ball than Nana Mama is probably mistaken.

Still, it was awesome to hear the ESPN guys talking about the Wildcats during their warm-up, and even better when they showed Damon on-screen.

"That's Damon Cross, who's been knocking down threes like nobody's business this season," one guy said. "I'm sure Coach Bolton has some high hopes for this sophomore starter from Washington DC."

Everyone went crazy when he said that, but Nana Mama made us all shut up when it was time for the tip-off.

Not that it stayed quiet for long. As soon as the Wildcats took possession, it was like a screaming contest in our living room. And when Damon grabbed a running pass and landed the first dunk of the night, it felt like the whole house was going to come down. He really did play like Curry, and I was hoping maybe Damon was headed for the NBA himself. How cool would that be? I don't think I've ever watched a game as closely as I was watching that one. In fact, I didn't even look down at my laptop until they went to the first commercial break.

But what I saw then changed everything.

The first thing I noticed on the computer was that it had a screen saver running. Which was weird. Usually, laptops just go to sleep to save the batteries. Not this one. It had a word rolling and bouncing around the screen.

Then I looked closer and saw that it wasn't a word, exactly. It was just a bunch of random letters: QUBUQ. Which is when I also realized, *no*. Those weren't just random letters. Not at all. QUB was Gabe's screen name in *Outpost*. And QUBUQ was the same thing, forward and backward.

It was also five letters long, which is exactly what I needed to get past that combination lock on the door to Gabe's bunker, inside the game.

Was I right? Was it really Gabe who broke in and stole our things? And then gave it back? Why would he do that? Where was he living, if he wasn't at home? What kind of trouble was he in?

So while some Geico ad played on the TV, and everyone else headed to the kitchen, or to the bathroom, I was sitting there completely zoned in on my computer.

This was no coincidence. That much I knew. It put a tingling, Spidey-sense kind of feeling right through me. Gabe wanted me to have this information, didn't he? And he made sure in his genius way that it would just be between the two of us. Why else would he go to all the trouble of smuggling it in to me like this?

In other words, I'd just gotten my first really big break in the case.

CHAPTER 24

MY HEART WAS making like a jackhammer in my chest by now, and my head was spinning around faster than that screen saver. I didn't know where this was leading, but one thing was for sure: I needed to get into *Outpost*, ASAP.

I still had the no-PlayStation rule from Dad, but that was like the least of my worries. The harder part was going to be getting to the basement without anyone knowing I was down there. At least I'd been sitting behind everyone so chances were good no one would look back and notice I wasn't there.

Once Damon's game was back on and everyone was re-glued to the TV, I ducked out the back of the living room and into the kitchen. If anyone saw, it was just going to look like I was getting something to eat.

I stood by the basement door after that, waiting for Davidson to score. When they did, everyone went crazy in the living room all over again, and I used the noise for cover. I eased open the door, stepped onto the stairs, and closed it again behind me.

About thirty seconds later, I was logging onto *Outpost* with the sound muted, just in case. The good news inside the game was that I'd already been to Gabe's home base once. That meant I could fast-travel there with one click now. It cost me half my energy reserves, but that didn't matter. I wasn't there to play.

Click.

As soon as I landed outside the bunker, I took a quick look around to see if anything was different this time. I made sure to look up, too, like Dad told me to do in the street that night. But I didn't see anything. No sign of any random players, and more important, no sign of Gabe. Not that I knew what to look for. He was already good at going unnoticed in real life. How hard would it be in a virtual world where he could make himself look like anything he wanted?

What really mattered right now was the fact that the clock was going *tick-tick-tick-tick*, and anyone might come looking for me at any second. I needed to get this done *now*. I didn't even have time to text the squad and tell them to log in with me.

I went to the bunker door and slid open the panel Ruby had found. Then I touched the keypad inside to bring it into close-up.

I typed in Q-U-B-U-Q. Took a deep breath. And hit Enter.

Right away, the screen changed. I could see Cassius Play from behind now, standing in front of the bunker door as it slid open. Yes!

Just then, another big yell came from upstairs. It sounded like the Wildcats were turning that game around. I really hated missing it, but there was zero chance I could stop what I was doing right now.

I stepped through the doorway.

Inside the bunker, all I saw was something that

looked like an old dusty storage unit. There were shipping containers, metal crates, and wooden boxes everywhere. Also, stacks of furniture and a bunch of stuff covered in tarps.

I'd been expecting some kind of dope bachelor pad, or a crazy high-tech lab, or I didn't even know what else. But not this. Which is why I knew there had to be more to it. This was Gabe, after all. No way he was going to bring me all this way for a dead end.

I started by clicking everything in sight. I touched every box, every piece of furniture, every section of wall, working my way from front to back. Still, nothing was happening. It was all just background art and I couldn't interact with any of it.

Not until I got to the very back of the room. I'd clicked about a hundred different things by then, but when I touched this one crate that looked like all the others, it slid off to the side. And right there in its place was a trap door with a recessed handle in the floor.

I knew it! And Gabe knew I'd find it, too. He knew I wouldn't give up on this. Just like I wasn't giving up on him.

When I lifted the trap, I saw a metal spiral staircase

winding down into the dark. I couldn't see where it was headed, so I pulled a flare off of Cassius Play's tool belt, lit it, and started down. The whole thing was legit creepy, like something out of movies Gabe and I had seen together. He was probably laughing his butt off about this somewhere. I'd kill him later. Just as soon as I made sure he was okay.

At the bottom of the stairs, I found another door. This one was unlocked, and the room on the other side was fully lit. That's where I found a crib like the one I'd been expecting from Gabe all along.

It looked like some kind of awesome penthouse apartment, minus the windows, since I was underground now. Gabe had it all decked out with virtual furniture, virtual rugs, and virtual electronics, although I wasn't going to be surprised if those electronics were functional, too. For all I knew, he'd figured out a way to put *actual* AV into this place, so he could come here and chill, or watch a movie, or whatever else he did with all that time he spent alone.

There was only one thing that looked out of place. At first, it seemed like some random yellow rectangle on the floor. But when I got closer, I saw it was an envelope. In *Outpost*, you can leave messages for anyone you want, as long as you play on the same server.

When I clicked the envelope, I expected it to come in close so I could open it, but that's not what happened. Instead, I got a pop-up with another message:

To continue, choose the correct answer.
WARNING: You will only have
one chance to get this right.

A) Did you know, you have your own Facebook group now?

B) Did you know, you have your own FB group now?

C) Did you know you have your own FB group now?

D) Did you know you have your own Facebook group now?

E) Did you know there's a FB group for you now?

F) Did you know there's a Facebook group for you now?

G) Did you know, there's a Facebook group for you now?

H) Did you know, there's a FB group for you now.

Oh, man! This, right here, was Gabe's genius in action.

What I had in front of me were a bunch of different versions of a text that I'd sent him. And now I was supposed to identify the version that showed an exact match. Which was information that only I could put my hands on.

Like I said—genius.

I pulled my phone out of my pocket, scanned through everything I'd sent him for the last sixteen days, and found exactly what I was looking for. Then I checked it against the versions he had up there on the screen, down to the last period and comma.

I double checked. Triple checked. And then I clicked on option D.

Right away, the pop-up window disappeared and that yellow envelope came back into view. While I watched, the envelope flapped open and a yellow page slid out, then came into close-up. It was a note, and all it said was—

BE BACK HERE
2 A.M. TONIGHT
SHARP

I almost shouted out loud when I saw that. This had to be from Gabe, didn't it? Just like the laptop clue and the passcode. But what did he mean, "be back here"? Was he going to show up? Is that what he'd been doing every night at 2:00 since he'd returned that laptop to my front porch? Or was he maybe surveilling my moves right now somehow?

I didn't have a whole lot of answers. In fact, I didn't have any. But there was one thing I knew for sure.

I knew exactly where I was going to be at 2:00.

CHAPTER 25

I **COULD BARELY** look at anyone when I got back to the living room. Lucky for me, nobody even noticed I'd been gone. Damon's game was off the hook, one of the best college ball head-to-heads I'd ever seen. Davidson had dropped behind Wake Forest in the first half but they came back hard in the second, and ended up winning, 89–82. Sixteen of those points were Damon's, too. He was tearing it up.

And maybe, just maybe, so was Gabe.

When I went to bed that night, I kept my phone

under the covers with the alarm set for 1:45 a.m. Which was like a joke. I mean, did I really think I'd be going to sleep any time before two? Yeah, right.

Instead, I just lay there, staring at the ceiling until it was finally time to sneak back to the basement. Then I soft-stepped down the quiet side of the stairs and stopped in the kitchen long enough to get a bowl of Rice Chex. Nana's room is right there, and I figured a midnight snack was the best alibi I could give, in case she got up to see who was prowling around.

But by 1:55 a.m., I was parked downstairs in front of my PS4. My hand was shaking on the controller as I logged in and got myself back over to Gabe's bunker. I used the QUBUQ entry code, made my way to the trap door, and went down the spiral stairs.

When I opened the door to the main part of Gabe's crib, it wasn't quite as empty as the last time. Someone else was there—another avatar. One I hadn't seen before. He was wearing an all-black superhero skin from head to foot, like Black Panther's or Venom's. It almost looked like a shadow standing there, but my mind was exploding with a pretty good idea of who this was.

I threw on my headset as fast as I could.

"Hello?" I said.

Which is when I heard Gabe's voice in my ear.

"Hey, man. What's up?"

I actually slapped a hand over my mouth just to keep from shouting, and waking up Nana. It was like fireworks going off in my brain. Like getting a full-body electric shock. Gabe Qualls was right there in front of me. As much as an avatar counts, anyway.

"Don't freak, okay?" he said. "I know this is crazy, but I just wanted to let you know I'm not cut up in pieces somewhere, or halfway to Alaska, like you might have been thinking."

Gabe didn't usually make a lot of jokes, but when he did, he had a weird sense of humor—even right now. As for me, I didn't know what to say. Which was crazy, since I'd been sitting on a giant pile of questions for sixteen days.

"Gabe…dude…I…Where are you?" I finally asked.

"It's better if we don't talk about that," Gabe said.

"Why? What's going on? Are you okay?"

"Listen," he said. "I don't have a lot of time. But I know you've been trying to find me, and I need to ask a huge favor."

"Anything. What is it?" I asked.

"Stop."

"What do you mean? Stop what?" I asked.

"Stop looking for me," Gabe said. "It's better if you do. For both of us."

"Slow down!" I said. I felt like I was on some kind of bullet train. Like everything was flying by so fast, I couldn't focus on any of it. "I need you to take about eight steps back—"

His avatar backed away from mine.

"Very funny," I said. "Seriously, Gabe, what the hell is going on?"

"It's complicated," he said.

"Is that why you broke into my house? Because it's complicated?" I asked. I didn't mean to sound mad. In fact, I didn't care that he'd done that. I just wanted to know why.

"I'm really sorry about that. I wish I could get

you all your stuff back, but I can't. It's too late for that."

"So, I know why you brought back the laptop, but what about the guns?" I asked.

"Those things freaked me out," he said.

"I knew it!" I said, too loud, and turned to look at the stairs to make sure nobody was coming. Then I went on, whispering again. "But why'd you take them in the first place?"

"Wasn't my choice," he said.

"What does that mean?" I asked.

"Listen," he said, "I wish I could tell you more, but I can't, okay?"

"Yeah, that's not good enough," I said. "Is this about your dad? Is he the reason you ran away?"

But Gabe wasn't biting on any of my questions. "Just one other thing," he said. "Did you tell anyone about this yet? I mean with your laptop and all?"

"No," I said. "It seemed like you wanted it to be a secret."

"Good," he told me. "Let's keep it that way. Total code of silence, okay? Not even Cedric, Ruby, or Mateo. And especially not your dad."

Now I was getting scared all over again. "Why, Gabe? Tell me something. Tell me anything, man," I said.

"If it gets too hot around here, I'm going to have to find a new spot, and then I don't know where I'd go," he said. "That's why you gotta quit looking for me. At least now I have..." He stopped for a second like maybe he'd said too much.

"At least now you have what?" I asked.

"Just promise you won't say anything. Please?"

I was feeling more desperate by the second, like this was only making things worse. But Gabe didn't sound so good, either.

"Okay, okay," I said. "I promise. But then, why did you even come here? Why are we having this conversation?"

"Because you're my only friend," Gabe said. "My only *real* friend, anyway. I didn't want you to worry."

That was almost like another joke. I was obviously going to worry now, more than ever.

"Are you coming back?" I asked. "Like, ever?" I knew I was asking too many questions, too fast, but I couldn't stop talking. "Gabe, listen. I can help you. Tell me what the problem is, or what I can do. I'll bring you whatever you need. Just say the word."

He didn't answer that one, either. It was silent for about five seconds, but his new avatar was still there, just standing like a statue. It didn't tell me much, except that he hadn't logged out.

"Gabe?" I tried again.

Then I heard another voice in the background. Not Gabe's. Somebody else. A guy. It was too muted to pick out any words, but it sounded like he was mad about something.

"Nothing," Gabe said then, but not to me. He was talking to whoever was there. "It's cool, I'm just...Chill, I'm just gaming."

I heard some more noise then. A shuffling sound. Maybe some kind of scuffle.

"Gabe!"

I felt totally helpless. It was like he was in trouble on the other side of some glass wall I couldn't reach through. I was *so* close, and there wasn't anything I could do.

"Get off me, man!" I heard him say then. "Just give me a second—"

Then it cut out. The sound stopped and the avatar in front of me blinked away, which meant Gabe had just logged off. Or someone had cut the power to the PlayStation.

I felt like I'd been kicked in the chest. I wanted to cry, shout, and punch something, all at the same time. Was he okay? Was he worse off than I thought?

Most important of all, how much time did I have left before Gabe disappeared again? He'd already proven he could do it once. Maybe he'd be even better at it the second time, and then I'd never hear from him again.

There was no way of knowing, but it sure seemed like I needed to pick up my pace now. It was like my dad says about his own investigations: The clock is *always* running.

And when it comes to a missing person, time is never on your side.

CHAPTER 26

FOR A LONG time, I stayed where I was, inside Gabe's bunker. I wanted to be there in case he came back, but I pretty much knew that wasn't going to happen. Still, I stuck to the basement couch, not going anywhere and watching the TV screen while I thought through everything that had just happened, about five times over. I didn't want to forget a single detail.

I also had to decide whether to keep my word and not tell anyone about this, or if it made more sense to break that promise, and hopefully help Gabe get home again. Half of my brain was shouting, "Keep it to yourself!" But the other half was more like, "Are you crazy?" This was a chance for the real detectives to track Gabe down. And protect him, too, in a way that I never could.

On the other hand, there was one thing I had that the cops didn't, and that was Gabe's trust. I couldn't just flush that away. The second I told Dad about any of this, I'd never be able to undo it. And the truth was, I didn't know *why* Gabe was so afraid of coming back. I decided to keep the whole conversation to myself for the time being, at least until I could think about it some more.

"Okay," I said to myself. "Fine. I'll keep your secret, Gabe. But there's no way I'm going to stop looking for you, especially now that I know something shady was going on. Guess again, son." This investigation was still on. More than ever.

Once I'd gotten that far, I dragged my butt off the couch, dumped my soggy Rice Chex in the kitchen, and went back to my room to keep working. It was around quarter to three by now, but I cracked my laptop and started writing a bunch of new notes, as fast as I could keyboard them in.

WHAT I KNOW
Gabe's alive
He's getting my texts
He's in the area
He has access to Outpost
Someone else is with him (at least one
    person; male)

WHAT I WANT TO KNOW
Why did Gabe run away?
Who is he with?
What does Mr. Qualls have to do with
    this (if anything)?
Is Gabe really robbing houses?
Where is he staying?

**WHY DOES HE WANT ME TO
STOP TRYING TO FIND HIM?**

Again, there was one item that jumped out at me
from the list I'd just made. It was the same thing
that kept circling back into my head every time I
thought about this stuff.

Mr. Qualls.

Gabe's dad was like my number one suspect now, even though I wasn't exactly sure what I suspected him *of*. He was living at home, but Gabe wasn't, according to the police. I just had a strong gut feeling that he had something to do with all this. My own dad always says his gut is the most valuable tool he has at work, and if it was good enough for him, it was good enough for me.

Also, I don't want to sound like I had a big head, but the truth was, I'd been right about Gabe all along, ever since that Christmas Eve burglary. Who was to say I didn't have Mr. Qualls pegged, too?

So for the second time since midnight, I got out of bed and snuck downstairs. Not for my PlayStation this time, but for Bree's laptop. I had some research to do, and if I wanted to do it right, this was the only way.

Technically, I was breaking a whole bunch of rules that night, but like Dad said before, I was in deep on this thing.

No stopping me now.

CHAPTER 27

I KNEW BREE'S work laptop was in her briefcase down in the front hall. And I knew she had an active Accurint account running on it, too.

Accurint is like Google on steroids. Cops use it all the time to look up information about suspects' criminal records, past employment, where someone's lived, and that kind of thing.

I parked myself on the bottom step by the hall table, opened Bree's briefcase, and took out her Toughbook. It was the perfect spot. If Bree or Dad came into the hall upstairs, or if Nana came out of her room, I'd hear them from either direction and have enough time to slip the laptop back where I found it.

I opened Bree's computer, clicked on the Accurint icon, and got straight to work.

I didn't even know Gabe's dad's first name, but there are all kinds of search fields you can use in there. So I put in everything I did know—Qualls; 17th Street SE; Washington, DC.

And that was enough. After I clicked Search, it gave me back a single matching record for those data points. Hopefully this was the right guy.

From there, I could choose to look at "Residential History," "Employment History," "Known Family," "Court Appearances," or "Criminal Arrests and Convictions."

I clicked on Criminal Arrests and Convictions. And just like that, I was staring at a mug shot for the guy I recognized as Mr. Qualls. He was looking right into the camera, and it creeped me out. How bad *was* this guy? Or, was I just letting my imagination get the best of me? It wouldn't have been the first time, that's for sure.

Mr. Qualls's first name was William. He also went by Dante, it said, which was his middle name. The page I was on showed three convictions that had resulted in prison sentences. Two of those were in Texas, from before Gabe was born. The most recent one was for aggravated robbery, right here in Washington, DC. He'd served four years of an eight-year sentence and had just gotten released in September.

I was shocked. Gabe had been an honest and good friend as long as I'd known him. Nothing like his dad. He had never said a word about any of this. Maybe that was some kind of clue and maybe it wasn't, but still, it felt like enough information to keep me moving in the same direction.

Once I'd read everything on that page, I dug a little deeper. Under Employment History, I saw that Mr. Qualls had mostly worked construction jobs in the past, but right now he was listed as unemployed.

I also learned that Mr. and Mrs. Qualls (her name was Virginia Johnson Qualls) had been married fourteen years. Before that, Mr. Qualls had two other sons, William Jr. and Ramon. Gabe had never mentioned them, either. Nothing about any half-brothers, or any family at all. I'd always figured he was just quiet that way. But maybe there was more to it than that.

Once I'd read through everything I could find, I navigated out of there, put back Bree's laptop, and went to my room to think about next moves.

It wasn't like I'd just discovered any big secrets. I knew Detective Sutter would have looked at all of this a long time ago. Maybe Mr. Qualls was a person of interest for her investigation, too. In fact, he probably was.

But that almost didn't matter either way. Because the next chance I got, I was going to be knocking on the Qualls's door again, to see what I could find out on my own.

CHAPTER 28

FINALLY, THAT TUESDAY at three thirty, my suspension was over. The timing was good, since the vigil for Gabe was that night. A whole lot of people showed up in front of the First Congregational Church at seven o'clock to lend their support. I went over with Nana, Jannie, Dad, and Bree. Cedric and his mom were there, and Mrs. Sandoval, too, handing out hot chocolate.

Ruby and Mateo's dad, Reverend Sandoval, was in charge of the whole thing. I stood on the sidewalk with my friends, handing out MISSING flyers while people started gathering.

I'd already decided I wasn't going to say anything to Ruby, Cedric, or Mateo about talking to Gabe. I was still keeping his secret that way, but otherwise, I was going to act like I'd been acting all along. That meant still looking for Gabe, still handing out those flyers, and also, telling my friends everything I was thinking about Mr. Qualls as soon as I got the chance.

Was I doing the right thing? Hard to say, since I was breaking someone's trust no matter what I did—either by saying more than Gabe wanted me to say, or by not saying enough to the three friends who had been in this with me from the beginning. It wasn't like there were any perfect choices, but I went with it.

Once the vigil started, Reverend Sandoval got up on the church steps and addressed the crowd. He led a couple of prayers and introduced the choir. They sang "Never Alone" while we all stood there in front of the church with candles. It was nice to see all these people who cared about Gabe come together like this. Even Detective Sutter was there.

She got up after that and thanked everyone for keeping an eye out for Gabe wherever they went.

Still, there was no denying the fact that it had been almost three weeks now. I'm not sure what anyone else was thinking, but Ruby, Mateo, and Cedric seemed pretty down about it.

"Feels like a dang funeral," Mateo said.

"Right?" Cedric said.

"Don't say that," Ruby told them. "It's bad luck." I could see she was trying not to cry, too. Which only made me feel worse about the eight-hundred-pound secret I was carrying on my back.

"I know Gabe's okay," I said. "He's not gone." And by that, I meant he wasn't dead, but I couldn't say it out loud.

"How can you be so sure?" Ruby asked. "You don't know if he's okay."

"I just have a feeling," I said. "Deep in my gut." Already, it was getting more complicated. I was going to have to watch what I said. And that's not exactly my specialty.

"I wish there was something else we could do," Cedric said.

"Actually, there is something," I told him. "I was thinking about going back over to Gabe's house on Saturday, and I could use a little backup."

Cedric nodded and put out a fist. I bumped him back, but people were also looking at us like we should shut up while the Reverend was giving his closing remarks.

We stopped talking, but even then, I wasn't hearing all of it. There was too much on my mind. On top of everything else, I was thinking about something Dad says happens all the time at crime scenes. The perps—people who are perpetrators of a crime—come around to watch the police work play out. Sometimes it gives them a kind of thrill. Other times, it's more about staying informed so they can be a step ahead of the authorities.

Not that this vigil was a crime scene. And not that Gabe was a criminal. But still, I wondered if the same idea applied. Was Gabe anywhere nearby, I wondered, just checking this all out? Or the guy he was arguing with while we were in *Outpost*?

While Reverend Sandoval talked, I scanned the area around the church. I checked the edges of the crowd, and the street corners just in sight. I looked in the windows of the apartments across the street, and in the dark doorways of the Christian Science reading room, and the hardware store, and the empty Chinese restaurant, too.

Are you here, Gabe? Watching? Right now?

It was the same question I'd had when I was in *Outpost*. Hiding in plain sight was Gabe's specialty. Like he was one part Harry Potter with that invisibility cloak, and one part Jason Bourne, from all those movies with Matt Damon. That character was always somewhere near the action, watching the people who were hunting him down, so he could figure out how to keep from being caught.

Maybe Gabe was doing his own version of the same thing. I wouldn't have put it past him, anyway. This was no game, but if it were, I'd say Gabe was winning, hands down. And I wasn't even sure anymore if that was a good thing or a bad thing.

CHAPTER 29

SATURDAY MORNING, I made an official plan with Cedric to do some gaming at his house. I also made an unofficial plan to meet him outside the Qualls's place before that. This was my chance to do a little more digging without anyone else knowing about it.

Cedric was like my man in the street, since this stuff was harder for Ruby and Mateo to get away with. He was also my backup, my extra muscle, and

189

maybe even my bodyguard, after what happened with Kahlil.

"I just need you to wait out here," I said when we got to Gabe's house. "It's safer if we're not both inside. I don't know what's going to happen, but if I'm not back in ten minutes, come and knock on the door."

Cedric didn't look too convinced. "You sure you know what you're doing?"

"Yeah," I said. "I'm looking for information about Gabe."

"Not what I meant," he said. "It just seems like maybe you're getting a little carried away with the whole detective thing. Don't be stupid in there, okay?"

"Sure. No stupider than usual," I said.

He gave me a grin for that one, but I knew he was serious, too. Then I crossed the street and went to knock on the door before he could try to talk me out of it.

I guess some part of me was expecting Mr. Qualls to answer like last time, because I was a little surprised when a lady opened the door.

"Uh, hi. Are you Mrs. Qualls?" I asked, even though I knew it was her. She had Gabe's big eyes, and a bunch of beaded dreads pulled back in a scarf. She was short, too, for a grownup. I guess Gabe inherited his size from his mom, not from his dad.

"Yes," she said. "Can I help you?"

"I'm a friend of Gabe's," I told her. "My name's Ali, and um..."

All kinds of thoughts were flashing through my mind now. It was a whole change-of-plans moment that happened in about half a second.

"I was here a couple weeks ago," I said, just rolling with it. "And I just wanted to come over and say I was sorry for bothering Mr. Qualls that day."

"Well, he's not here right now," she told me. "So don't you worry about it. The truth is, Gabe doesn't have a lot of friends. It's sweet of you to stop by."

So maybe I couldn't interview Mr. Qualls, but I still had an opportunity to get something done here.

"Is there any chance I could see Gabe's room?" I asked. "I know that might sound weird, but—"

"Oh, honey, of course," she said. I could tell she thought I wanted to see it to help me feel better, not because I was investigating anything. But I wasn't going to spell it out for her.

"Thanks," I said, as she opened the door wider. "I really appreciate this."

I gave Cedric one last look over my shoulder. He was standing there eating a Kudos bar and looking confused, but I just kept moving.

The inside of the house was as depressing as the outside. The curtains were closed and a couple of big candles were burning. It smelled like cinnamon and cigarette smoke in there. A big glass ashtray was overflowing with butts on the coffee table, and someone had punched a hole in the wall at some point. I was pretty sure I knew who, too.

I tried to take it all in like a detective and not get too sucked into anything else about it.

"Have you heard anything from the police?" I asked, as casually as I could. "Any new word about Gabe, or whatever else?"

Mrs. Qualls shook her head, but just barely, like it hurt to think about it. "Not a word," she said. I felt really sorry for her. She was obviously feeling low, and she didn't have to let me in like this.

"You can throw your coat right there, if you like," she said, pointing at a chair by the door. It was pretty hot and stuffy in there, so I took her up on that and then followed her up some narrow stairs to the second floor.

Gabe's bedroom door had a big Fuse ODG sticker on it, and the knob had been broken off at some point. The room itself was really small. It had one little window looking out to 17th Street, and I could see Cedric pacing around outside. He looked up just then, and gave me a look, like, *What the heck, bro?* But it wasn't like I was going to start sending him hand signals, so I turned away.

The bed took up most of the room, but there was also a TV on the floor and a wire rack with some clothes piled on it. There wasn't a closet or dresser. No books. Not much of anything else, really, unless you counted all the *Outpost* screen captures he'd printed out and tacked up on the wood paneling— more of his own virtual inventions and other stuff he'd built in the game.

"Is there any chance I could get onto Gabe's PlayStation for a minute?" I asked. I wanted to see if it told me when he'd last used it, or anything else.

"Oh, that's gone," she said, and pointed at the space on the floor next to the TV. "It's the one thing Gabriel took with him."

"He did?" I asked, while my thoughts went flying all over again. That explained what had been weighing down Gabe's backpack that day. So he'd been planning to leave home since at least the morning, when he packed it up, but he never said a word about it that day. I guess I shouldn't have been surprised he took his PS4 with him. Gabe loved that thing more than anything else.

Still, he had to have it hooked up somewhere. That meant electricity, and internet. He couldn't just be squatting in some deserted building, even though that's what I'd been imagining.

This also meant that his parents knew from the start that Gabe had run off on purpose, and that he hadn't been kidnapped, or whatever else. In which case, Detective Sutter would have known it, too. It wasn't like I'd expected Sutter to tell me everything she knew, but it did make me wonder what else they hadn't shared. I guess we all had our own secrets.

I was back over by the window now, and I stole another quick look at Cedric. Except this time, I could see something was wrong. He was still standing on the sidewalk across the street, looking agitated, but when he saw me, it kicked up a notch. He was mouthing something and pointing really hard back my way, toward the front of Gabe's house.

For a second, I was like, *huh?* But only until I looked down and saw Mr. Qualls! Already, he was coming up the front steps. And even though he was the person I'd been hoping to speak with that morning, something in my gut told me that Mr. Qualls wasn't going to like finding me already inside, much less in his son's room, poking around.

And it turns out, I was absolutely right about that.

CHAPTER 30

"HELLO?" MR. QUALLS called out. "Whose jacket is this?"

"We're up here," Mrs. Qualls said, just before I heard feet on the stairs.

All of a sudden, I got a fresh whiff of cigarette smoke, and then Mr. Qualls was there. He stood in the door, blocking my way out, holding a cigarette between his lips and staring at me like I didn't belong.

"What's going on in here?" he asked.

"This is Gabe's friend," Mrs. Qualls said.

"That so?" he asked, like he didn't believe her. Or maybe more like, he didn't believe me.

Suddenly, this whole visit seemed like a really bad idea. I didn't know what was going to happen, but I just wanted to get out. It wasn't like Cedric was going to come crashing in to give me some backup, as much as I wished he would. Besides, Mr. Qualls was more than big enough to deal with both of us. I should have thought of that, too.

"I didn't mean any disrespect," I said. "I just came to—"

"Did I or did I not tell you to go home the last time, boy?" Mr. Qualls asked. "Who you think you are, barging in here? I know what you're trying to do, and I won't have it."

"Dante, take it easy," Mrs. Qualls said, but he wasn't listening to her.

"Nah," he said, right at me. "I've had just about enough of you. This is *my* home. *My* rules. You hear?"

I couldn't look away from Mr. Qualls, but I badly wanted to signal to Cedric to help me out. I wouldn't have minded taking a quick exit out that window, either. But no chance there.

Mr. Qualls came right at me, took me by the arm, and basically dragged me out of the room. I had to step quick to keep from tripping, including on the stairs.

A second later, he was throwing open the door and shoving me outside. I stumbled down the front steps.

"Yo! Leave him alone!" Cedric said. He was coming over now.

"Don't make me do something I'm gonna regret," Mr. Qualls said, pointing a finger right at me from the door.

"For god's sake, Dante, give the boy his coat." Mrs. Qualls was there now, too, holding it out for me. Mr. Qualls snatched it off of her and threw it down the steps.

"We're done here," he said. "You got me?"

He didn't wait for an answer, either. He slammed the door, and just like that, it was over.

Cedric was right there now, handing me my coat off the ground. "You okay?" he asked, while we moved away from the house. I wasn't going to run. I didn't want to give Mr. Qualls the satisfaction, even if I was shaking all over.

And I was wondering, more than ever, just what Gabe's dad might be hiding. Because as dumb as my own moves might have been that day, I was more convinced than ever that he was making a few mistakes of his own.

Something was definitely up with that guy. I didn't know what it was, but I still intended to find out.

ALEX CROSS

IT WAS EARLY Sunday morning when Alex Cross got another text from Detective Olayinka.

OLAYINKA: Hey Alex. You awake?

CROSS: Yeah, what's up?

OLAYINKA: Another robbery in your neighborhood. Two of them, actually, sometime in the last 24 hours. But I need to talk to you about one in particular.

CROSS: Sure. Any details?

OLAYINKA: Best to talk in person if that's okay. We're just around the corner from you, on Ellen Wilson Place. Can't miss us.

OLAYINKA: You free right now?

Alex was glad to be included in anything to do with this case. But Olayinka's air of urgent mystery, or whatever this was, didn't sit well. What could Isaac have to say that couldn't go in a text or be told in a phone call?

There was one quick way to find out, anyway.

The house Olayinka had mentioned was even closer than the last robbery on 4th Street. Alex walked around the block to 6th, then cut in on Ellen Wilson Place, a small alley of a side street with some surprisingly well-to-do homes along its narrow passage.

He found the detective waiting for him outside, while several other personnel came and went through the front door of a three-story brick house, lit up on all levels from the inside.

"What's going on?" Alex asked. It seemed odd for the lead detective to station himself out there. Something had changed, Alex thought. He could feel it on a gut level. And the last thing he needed that morning was one more complication.

"I'm sorry to pull a move on you," Olayinka said.

"But I just wanted to show you this first, off the record, before it goes in for evidence. We found it on the back steps, where someone jimmied the door."

Olayinka pulled a small, clear evidence baggie from his puffy down coat pocket and held it out to show. It looked like the bag held a credit card, or ID of some kind.

"What is it?" Alex asked. "And why do I think I'm not going to like this?"

"Just take a look," Olayinka told him, handing over the sealed evidence.

As Alex peered closer, he saw it was in fact a student ID card from Washington Latin Middle School. The sight of it sent his pulse spiking, even before he'd turned the card over. And there on the front was Ali's name and picture. If he hadn't been staring at it himself, Alex might not have believed what he was seeing.

"This has to be some kind of mistake," he said.

"I'm hoping so, too," Olayinka answered, taking the evidence and sliding it back into his pocket. "But I just wanted you to know, we're going to have to consider this one very seriously. And we're going to want to talk to your son."

CHAPTER 31

DAD WAS SHAKING me awake, again. It was Sunday morning, and I was wondering if we were going out to breakfast like the last time.

"What's up?" I asked. "We going somewhere? 'Cause I'm starving."

"Where were you yesterday afternoon?" Dad asked. And the way he asked it, I knew in less than a second that something bad had happened.

"How come?" I asked, but he only looked back at me. The ball was in my court to answer, and we both knew it. "I was hanging out with Cedric," I said.

"Are you sure about that?" Dad asked. "And will Cedric be sure about it when the *police* ask him?"

I was awake now. Wide awake.

"Dad, what's going on?" I asked.

"Detective Olayinka wants to speak with you," he said. "They found your school ID at the site of another robbery. One that could have happened anytime in the last twenty-four hours."

I couldn't believe what I was hearing. It was like it didn't even make sense.

"But...I have my ID," I said. "It's in my coat pocket."

"Let's see," Dad asked.

I was up in a second, and ran down the stairs to the hooks by the front door. I reached into the right pocket of my coat, where I always kept my ID and my house key. But all I found there was the key.

I tried the left pocket after that, but it was empty. Same thing for every other pocket in that coat, and the more I checked, the bigger that pit in my stomach started to get.

Dad was watching me from the bottom of the stairs. "Nothing?" he asked.

"It must have dropped out," I said, and at the same second, I realized *where* it must have dropped out. Back at the Qualls's house. Which meant I had a whole lot of explaining to do. A lot of coming clean, too. It was like everything I'd been building up all this time was about to come crashing down, and I couldn't do anything to stop it anymore.

"We've got a lot to talk about," Dad said.

"I didn't break into any houses, I swear!" I cried. I was trying not to panic, but it felt like I was running away from an avalanche.

"If that's what you say, then I believe you," Dad told me. "But something tells me there's more to the story here."

I felt like I'd just stumbled into a brand-new nightmare. And as impossible as it seemed, it was also clear to me what was going down here.

Mr. Qualls was trying to frame me for robbery.

CHAPTER 32

INSTEAD OF GOING back to Youth Services like the last time, Dad took me to the Daly Building on Indiana Avenue. That's police headquarters in Washington, where Detective Olayinka worked, and where Dad's office was, too.

The lobby of that building is this huge, high-ceilinged place that echoes as you walk through. It always feels like something out of Gotham City to me. I could see Batman facing down the Joker in a place like that.

But not us. We had a different kind of face-off. With the press. I guess they always hung out there, looking for a story. So they moved in on Dad as soon as we came through the revolving doors. Not because they were expecting us, but because Dad's trial was starting the next day.

"Detective Cross! How are you feeling about tomorrow?"

"Have you apologized to the Yang family, Alex?"

"Alex, over here! Just a few questions!"

I already felt bad, dragging Dad down there. But now I felt even worse. The last thing he wanted that day was a face full of reporters.

"Hey, Ali!" one of them called out while we moved toward the security station. "What are you doing here with your father?"

Dad put a hand on my shoulder. I knew what it meant, too. *Just keep moving.* But he didn't have to worry about me this time. I'd learned my lesson the hard way, and I knew these people weren't asking real questions. They just wanted something that would make people click on their stories or buy their papers.

Besides, I had way bigger things to worry about right now.

"No comment," I said to all those reporters.

Some people laughed, like it was funny for a kid to say that. But I didn't care. Dad gave me a proud-of-you squeeze and steered us toward the metal detectors.

The press wasn't allowed past security, but they kept calling out questions while I emptied my pockets into a white plastic bowl and put it on a conveyor belt. Then I stepped through the scanner and waited for Dad to do the same thing.

"Detective Cross?"

"Any last words for us, Alex?"

"Alex, over here!"

Neither one of us said a word. Not until we were on the elevator and heading up to the fourth floor. Then Dad kind of leaned into me, the way he does when he's trying to cheer me up.

"Good job," he said. "I'm sure that wasn't easy for you."

"Easier than you think," I told him.

Because the fact was, the hard part was just ahead of me, not behind.

Chapter 33

THE NEXT SURPRISE was seeing Detective Sutter in the fourth-floor bull pen when we got there. She was waiting for us along with Detective Olayinka, and it only took me a second to realize that this was actually good news. If Sutter and Olayinka were both interested in these robberies, that meant I was right about Gabe having something to do with it.

It also meant twice the law enforcement out there looking for my friend.

But meanwhile, I had some hot water to get out

of. Technically, and maybe officially, I was a suspect now.

They brought us into one of those little interview rooms, just like the last time at Youth Services. The only difference was that the red light on the ceiling camera was lit. Which felt extra weird. If they were recording this meeting, did that mean someone was going to watch it later and analyze my answers? And did *that* mean I had to be even more careful about what I said?

Sure, no pressure.

"Are you guys working together on the Gabe Qualls case?" I asked once we sat down.

Sutter and Olayinka looked at each other. They didn't say anything, but I could see the *yes* in their expressions.

"Ali, we're going to keep it focused this time," Detective Sutter said. "We won't be answering any questions for you today."

My knee was bouncing like crazy, and Dad put a hand on it under the table to stop me. I was nervous, for sure. Not just about what they were going

210

to ask, but also about everything I knew I had to tell them now.

Olayinka went first. "So, how do you think your school ID got to the back steps of that house?"

"I can't prove anything," I said, "but if you ask me, Mr. Qualls put it there. That guy is *shady*, with a capital *S*."

"And what makes you say that?" Olayinka asked.

"Well..."

Here it went. I hadn't even told Dad the story yet. I hadn't had the nerve to bring it up in the car, and I knew he was going to find out about it soon enough. Like right now. I told them about the laptop, and the conversation I'd had with Gabe inside his bunker, in *Outpost*. Then I told them about what happened when I went to the Qualls's house, and how Mr. Qualls threw my coat out the door like he had.

"He either stole my ID out of my pocket, or it fell out when he threw the coat," I said. "Either way, he's the only person who had a chance of getting it off of me."

Olayinka sat back and gave me a look that I didn't like so much.

"That's quite a big story, on the same day you've been implicated in this," he said. "Why didn't you come forward as soon as you spoke with Gabe?"

"Because Gabe asked me not to," I said.

It was like someone had just turned up the heat in that little room. The back of my neck was itchy, and my knee was going again. Did they think I was trying to lie my way out of this?

"I wanted to protect him," I kept going. "But I was also trying to figure out what I was protecting him *from*. That's why I was investigating his dad. Mr. Qualls has *something* to do with this. I just don't know what it is yet."

"Didn't you tell your father that you thought Gabe was part of these robberies?" Sutter asked me.

"Yeah?" I said, looking at Dad. I guess they'd been talking about it. "But there's some reason that's making him do it, I'm positive."

"And now you're saying Mr. Qualls is also involved somehow?" Sutter asked. "Even though Gabe is missing?"

"That's the weird part," I said. "I haven't really figured it out yet."

I saw the way they'd looked at each other when I used the word "investigating," and it ticked me off, to be honest. I knew my investigation wasn't real compared to theirs, but the fact was, I'd learned a thing or two since I started, including a few things even they didn't know until I told them.

"Where did you go after you left the Qualls's house?" Olayinka asked.

"To Cedric's," I said. "We hung out, talked about the Gabe stuff, and played some *Outpost*. Then I came home for dinner."

Sutter was still scribbling notes.

"And were you home all night?" Olayinka asked.

"Yes," I said.

"Can you vouch for him?" Olayinka asked Dad. "Or is it possible he could have snuck out?"

"Oh, come on," Dad said, but Olayinka just waited, and Dad went on. "I was asleep, so if I had to swear, then no. I can't say for sure."

"Has he ever snuck out before?"

Dad looked at me again. "Have you?"

"Maybe," I said. "I mean, yeah. But I didn't sneak out last night, I swear!"

"I believe you," Dad said, and looked at the detectives.

"Okay." Sutter closed her notebook. "I think that's everything we need for now."

A minute later, we were on our way out of there. I didn't know if I'd just gotten myself in deeper, or if I was in the clear, or what. But there was one thing that kept scratching at my brain all the way home. It was something Gabe said to me when I talked to him online that night. He'd said it would be better "for both of us" if I stopped trying to find him.

For both of us?

I didn't think about it at the time, but now it made a whole new kind of sense. Because Mr. Qualls was nobody you wanted to mess with, and that was as true for Gabe as it was for me.

I could see it clearly, now. And just about a day too late.

CHAPTER 34

IN THE CAR, Dad let me have it.

"We need to talk about this detective work of yours," he told me. "Mr. Qualls might be dangerous, which you already knew. In fact, it concerns me more than anything that you *did* know that and you still went back to the house."

"I brought Cedric," I said. "I didn't go by myself."

"Do you really think that's going to make me feel any better?" Dad asked. "It just puts two of you in a place that you shouldn't be. This isn't a game, Ali."

"I know that!" I shouted back. As soon as it came out, I felt sorry for yelling, but it was too late to stop. This whole thing was spilling up and out of me now, like it or not.

"Gabe's my friend!" I said. "And it's like nobody cares. I mean, I know they're doing their jobs, but it's been three weeks. *More* than three weeks! And I'm the only person who's actually talked to him. You want to know the truth, Dad? It shouldn't be that way. Those detectives should be doing their jobs and finding him. Why is it taking so long? Why isn't anyone..."

My throat closed around the words before I could finish. I wasn't even seeing straight. Then my eyes filled up with water.

"Why isn't anyone finding my friend?" I asked.

Dad pulled over in front of an apartment building on 3rd Street and put the car in park.

"Come here," he said. He gave me a big hug, and I kind of emptied out, crying as hard as I ever have. I was just really, really stressed. And I was sad that my friend wasn't getting the attention he deserved.

"I'm sorry," I said. "I didn't mean that about the police."

"Nothing to be sorry for," Dad told me. Then he sat back and looked at me across the seat. "You want to know something? I was so angry about how a case was going one time, I punched a mirror in the bathroom at work. I even cried that day."

"You *did*?" I asked. It was a lot easier for me to imagine Dad punching something than it was to imagine him crying. Not that he's some super-tough Luke Cage kind of guy. But at the same time, he *is* pretty tough.

"One of the hard things about this work is not taking the job too personally," Dad said. "Most days, I can do that. But every once in a while? Not so much."

I'd talked to Dad about his job a million times, but he'd never said any of this before.

"You have everything it takes, Ali," Dad went on. "If you want to be a real detective someday, then that's exactly what you're going to be. It's when you *stop* caring that you have to worry."

I wasn't crying anymore, but there were still tears on my cheeks, and I wiped them on my sleeve. I took one of those shaky breaths and tried to refocus while Dad pulled away from the curb. Then we were driving again.

"Thanks, Dad," I said.

"In the meantime, I'm putting you on hold," he told me. "No more investigation on this one. No more going anywhere near the Qualls's house. And no more secrets. You have a tendency to go all in, Ali. There's no halfway for you, and that makes me nervous. Actually, no, it terrifies me."

"It does?" I was learning all kinds of new stuff about Dad.

"Yes, it does," he said. "We have one missing kid already. I will not take any chances on you becoming the next one. No more of this investigation for you. Got it?"

"Yes, sir," I said. "I got it."

But at the same time, I wasn't 100 percent sure I was making a promise I could keep.

CHAPTER 35

THAT NIGHT, I met Cedric, Mateo, and Ruby in *Outpost* for a gaming session. But also a truth session.

"Look out!"

"I'm looking! Where are they?"

"Straight up!"

I looked up and saw a squadron of ultralights with flamethrowers passing right over the tree-top base station where Lowkey-Loki, Blackhawk, Cagey-B, and I had taken up a position. A column of fire shot right at me and I had to drop down to the lower branches just to avoid getting flamed right out of the game.

"We're not going to be able to hold this," Ruby said. I looked again and saw the three of them returning fire, but the treehouse itself was burning up. Flaming branches and pieces of lumber were falling past me already.

"We need to ditch!" Cedric said.

"Guess I'll have to rebuild that treehouse," Mateo said. Like that didn't happen all the time. The whole point of the game wasn't about staying in one place. It was about adapting.

A few minutes later, we'd all reconvened on the beach, with a huge lake spread out in front of us. Ruby had already requisitioned a sweet-looking airfoil, too, so we hopped on and headed for another shore.

"Hey, listen, you guys," I said. "I need to catch you up." I'd been putting it off, because I didn't know how they'd react to this, but the longer I waited, the worse it was going to get. Also, it seemed easier to do this over a headset instead of face-to-face.

"What's up? Something with Gabe?" Ruby asked.

"Yeah," I said. "A whole lot, actually."

"What about him?"

I counted to five, just to make sure I still wanted to do this.

"I talked to him," I said. "A week ago."

"Say *what*?" Mateo asked.

"How?" Cedric asked.

"Inside *Outpost*," I said. "He tracked me down. I got the entry code for his bunker, and he left me a message about when to meet. Which is what we did."

"Hang on, hang on, hang on," Cedric said. "What do you mean, *meet*?"

I could tell they weren't exactly pumped about the fact that I'd been keeping secrets. But I couldn't stop now, they had to hear it all.

"I mean, he logged in as some other avatar, just like you thought he might. And we met in that bunker," I said. "He wanted someone to know he was okay, or at least...you know. Not gone."

Not dead is what I meant, but I didn't want to say that.

Now I felt like an idiot for holding back this long, even though at the same time, I would have felt just as bad if I'd broken my promise to Gabe right away.

"I'm not saying it was the right thing to do," I told them. "I don't know if there *was* a right thing. I was just trying to see if I could get a few things figured out first—"

Ruby cut me off. "Whatever, Ali," she said. "I'm out."

"What do you mean, *out*?" I asked. But then Blackhawk disappeared from the screen in front of me. She'd been the one driving that airfoil, and it spun out now and came to a stop on the water.

"Mateo, tell her to get back online," I said. "At least let me explain."

But that's as far as I got with him, too. On-screen, I saw Cagey-B turn to face Cassius Play. Then he raised his plasma and fired, point blank.

"Whoa! Whoa! Whoa!" I said, too late. He'd already vaporized me right out of the game.

"What'd you do that for?" I asked him, but he didn't answer.

"Mateo just bounced," Cedric told me. "I'm in here by myself now."

"I'll log back in," I said. "Be right there."

"Don't worry about it," Cedric told me. "I'm gonna go."

"Come on, man. You, too?" I asked. I thought if anyone was going to understand how this was for me, it would be Cedric. But I guess not. It felt more like I was circling the drain, going down, down, down.

"I'm not mad," Cedric said. "Not like those guys. It's just...I don't know, bro. I'm not really sure what to think."

In other words, he *was* mad.

"Yeah, okay. Text me if you want to get back on," I told him.

"Sure," he said, even though we both knew that wasn't going to happen.

Then he disconnected, and I just sat there, feeling as alone as I'd felt since this whole crazy, stupid situation started. I'd basically messed this up for myself by keeping secrets—from the police *and* my friends. Then, I'd messed it up even more by telling the truth. I seriously didn't know where that left me, or what I was supposed to do about it now.

Whatever it was, though, I'd be doing it on my own.

ALEX CROSS

"ALL RISE FOR the honorable Judge Felicity Lautner," the bailiff called out, and everyone rose to their feet.

The judge, a tall white woman with a lace collar on her robe, smiled curtly out at the room as she ascended to the bench.

"Please be seated," she said. Alex took his seat, and then a deep breath, too. Next to him was Deirdre Tennant, his criminal attorney. As much as it was possible to be ready for something like this, they were.

The Washington DC Superior Court was in a vast, white concrete building next to MPD headquarters on Indiana Avenue. Alex had been here dozens of times, if not hundreds. But never like this. The grim look on Bree's and Nana's faces said it all as they sat quietly waiting. This trial couldn't be over soon enough.

On the other side of the room, June and Melissa Yang, the wife and daughter-in-law of Stanley Yang, sat nearer the prosecutor's table. A seven-woman, five-man jury was seated on the far wall, under a large vintage photo of the Washington Monument.

"Let me thank you all ahead of time for your efficiency," Judge Lautner began. "I've looked over the briefing documents, and don't expect this should take more than a few days to complete."

Alex was glad to hear it. DC judges were notoriously cautious about having their cases overturned on appeal, and most preferred to take their time. Trials in Washington generally took longer than anywhere in the country. But not on Judge Lautner's watch.

After Ms. Tennant entered Alex's not-guilty plea

and both lawyers made their opening statements, the Yangs' attorney, Robert Sheinken, called his first witness.

It began with an assistant medical examiner who had responded to Mr. Yang's fall on that fateful day in June. Under Mr. Sheinken's questioning, the AME reported that the bruises found on Mr. Yang's arms could easily have come from some kind of tussle or struggle before he'd fallen.

On cross-examination, however, Alex's lawyer, Deirdre Tennant, got the doctor to freely admit that those bruises could have also come from the fall itself.

Up next, Mr. Yang's wife, June, testified in a halting voice about hearing an argument on her front porch that day. As far as she could tell, she said, Alex had been aggressive from the moment he'd arrived, and then rude and dismissive when she'd come outside to find her husband unconscious on the sidewalk.

Alex's heart clenched as she spoke. He'd been giving CPR to Mr. Yang when his wife came out, and yes, it was entirely possible that he'd come off as rude in the moment. Still, it was hard to watch this woman in so much pain, even as she testified against him. If nothing else, the fact that she hadn't actually seen Mr. Yang's fall meant her testimony was only worth so much to the prosecution.

Finally, Alex himself was called to the stand. He wasn't required by law to give testimony. The Fifth Amendment guaranteed that. But it was important to Alex that Jannie, Damon, and Ali know he had nothing to hide. He *wanted* the court to hear his story, and his legal team had reluctantly agreed.

Once Alex was sworn in, Robert Sheinken adjusted his red-striped power tie, stood up, and walked slowly toward the witness stand.

"Detective Cross," he said, "can you describe what happened on the afternoon of June thirtieth in front of Stanley Yang's home?"

"Sure," Alex answered. He'd been over it in his mind every day for the last six months. There was no forgetting it now. "I came to ask Mr. Yang a few follow-up questions about his son's murder charge. When I got there, Mr. Yang was understandably upset, and things turned tense very quickly. Then, as he came out through the screen door, he pushed me straight back. I remember that I stumbled, and I took three steps toward the stairs."

"And you didn't fall," the attorney said.

"No," Alex answered. "But Mr. Yang continued to advance on me at that point—"

"Where was your police weapon?"

"Holstered at my side," Alex answered.

"Okay. Please continue."

"Mr. Yang advanced, and I stepped to my right, to get out of his way—"

"Excuse me?" Mr. Sheinken interrupted. "You were at the very top of the porch stairs as Mr. Yang came toward you, and you *stepped aside*?" He spoke the last two words as though stepping aside were a crime and not a normal impulse.

"That's right," Alex answered. "Mr. Yang was quite agitated, and—"

"Did it occur to you that he might not have seen the stairs behind you?"

"Not in that moment, no," Alex answered. "It all happened in a second, maybe two. That's when Mr. Yang lurched forward and fell off the porch."

"How far from him were you at this point?"

"Not far. Maybe two feet," Alex asked.

"Would you say you were less than an arm's reach away?" Sheinken stepped toward the witness stand and extended his hand until it was just shy of Alex's chest. "This close?"

"Yes, I'd say so," Alex answered. He knew where the attorney was going with this. There was nothing to do but tell the truth.

"And what kept you from reaching out to grab Mr. Yang, or to stop him from making that fall?" Sheinken asked.

"I did reach," Alex answered. "If my reflexes had been a fraction of a second faster, we wouldn't be here today."

The prosecutor turned to face the jury now. "And did you touch him in any way, Detective Cross?"

"My hand brushed off his arm," Alex answered.

"So it's possible that as you reached out, you may have even *pushed* him," he said.

"Objection, your honor!" Deirdre Tennant was on her feet now. "Mr. Sheinken is wildly speculating here."

"Sustained," Judge Lautner answered from the bench. "Mr. Sheinken, would you care to rephrase that?"

Robert Sheinken didn't miss a beat. "My point, Detective Cross, is that you showed up at the Yangs' home as an officer of the law. You initiated a conversation you *knew* would upset Mr. Yang, and yet—"

"Objection! Is there a question here?" Tennant called out.

Judge Lautner gave a stern glance to the prosecutor. "Is there, Mr. Sheinken?"

"Yes, ma'am. I'm just about there," Sheinken answered, and turned on Alex again. "You engaged in a contentious conversation with Mr. Yang, by your own description. And at that charged and emotional moment, you failed to protect Mr. Yang when he came toward you. In fact, Detective Cross, you cleared the way for Stanley Yang to fall down those stairs. So my question is simply this: Is all of that accurate?"

Alex resisted the temptation to grit his teeth in front of the jury. Robert Sheinken knew exactly what he was doing.

"Detective?" he prodded.

"That's physically accurate, but it has nothing to do with my intention," Alex answered. "I wish I'd been able to stop that fall, but I couldn't."

"I see," Sheinken said, as he turned away once more. This last part was just for the jury. "So while I can't prove malicious intent here, it does seem to me that you had everything you needed to keep Mr. Yang safe, Detective Cross—"

"Your honor!" Tennant called out. "At what point does this monologue end? Is Mr. Sheinken auditioning for a movie or making his case?"

"That's quite enough, Mr. Sheinken," the judge said.

"I'm done, your honor. No further questions," the attorney said, and walked back to his table without another glance. The twelve jurors, likewise, seemed to avoid Alex's eyes when he looked over.

Maybe testifying had been a mistake. Maybe even a fatal one. The sense of it dropped like a stone into Alex's gut.

But it was too late to take it back now.

CHAPTER 36

I **KIND OF** zombied my way through school the next morning. Dad's trial was starting, I was at least technically a robbery suspect, Gabe was still out there, and I was getting the silent treatment from my friends. Let's just say that math, English, and social studies weren't the first things on my mind that day.

At lunch, when I came off the line with my tray, I saw Ruby, Cedric, and Mateo at our usual table. I wanted to just turn the other way and go eat with the Spanish Club in Mr. Egan's room. But when Cedric spotted me, it felt too weird to not at least walk over.

"Hey," I said.

"Hey," Cedric said, kind of quietly, like he was shy or something. Which isn't Cedric at all.

Ruby didn't even look up. She just pushed some tater tots around her tray with her fork while I stood there feeling stupider by the second. Basically, I'd broken my promise to Gabe *and* made these guys mad at the same time. Talk about a lose-lose.

"Listen, I'm really sorry about how it all went down," I said.

"Why would you keep something like that from us?" Mateo finally spoke up.

"Because Gabe asked me to," I said. "I don't know why, but he did."

"You're the one who pulled us into this thing," Mateo said. "Remember?"

"Come on, man, give him a break," Cedric said, but without looking at me.

"I didn't even tell the police until I had to," I said. "And then first chance I got, I told you guys, too. It's not like—"

"Not like what?" Ruby asked. Now she *was* looking at me and I almost wished she'd stop. "Not like you let us keep wondering if Gabe was even alive? Not like you stood there and watched me cry at that vigil? Oh, wait. That's *exactly* what you did."

I couldn't blame her for being mad. She'd done more to help find Gabe than anyone, except for me. I just didn't know how to fix it.

"Anyway," I said. "I wanted you all to know that I'm going to keep looking, and I'll give you a heads-up if I find anything new...."

I couldn't even finish. I might as well have been talking to the floor.

"And I guess that's it," I said. "So...I'll see you guys later."

"See you," Cedric said. "Don't do anything stupid out there, man."

"Too late," I said. It was supposed to be a joke, but nobody laughed. Instead, I just took my tray, dumped my lunch in the trash, and left the cafeteria.

Then, because my day wasn't already bad enough, who do I see in the hall but Kahlil Weyland. Of course.

"Look who it is. Sherlock Homie," he said, and laughed like he'd made the world's greatest joke. Then he just stood there, blocking my way.

"What do you want, Kahlil?" I asked.

"Nothing," he said, like he meant it, which I knew he didn't. "I was just wondering if what I heard was true."

I didn't say anything. I wasn't going to give him the satisfaction of asking what he meant, but he kept going anyway.

"I heard you've been doing a little breaking and entering on the side," he said. "My dad told me they found your school ID at a—"

"Yeah, well, your dad's wrong," I said, cutting him off. "And I guess he's got just as big a mouth as you do."

I was over it. I didn't care what Kahlil said, and I kind of didn't care what he did, either.

Just like that, he was in my face all over again. His chest was up and out, pushing into me, close enough that I could smell his nasty breath, too.

"You really want to do this?" he asked.

"Nah," I said. "I really don't."

"Yeah, without your little friends around to protect you, I can see why not."

"You can't see anything," I said.

"What's that supposed to mean?"

He didn't even deserve an explanation. But now that I'd started, the rest of it just rolled out of me.

"See, here's what I figured out about me and you," I said. "We're kind of alike."

Kahlil laughed again and sprayed some more of that bad breath all over me. "I don't think so," he said.

"No, we really are," I said. "It's like when either one of us gets onto something, we're just a dog with a bone, and we don't let go."

I think he was actually confused now. Like he didn't know whether to laugh, walk away, or punch me.

"What are you even talking about?" he asked, and pushed me hard. This dude liked to fight, for sure, but I meant what I'd said. So I stood my ground and kept talking instead.

"See, the difference is, all you want to do is beef with me and make trouble. Which I don't even get, by the way. Like seriously, why do you even care so much?"

I think that one stumped him, but I wasn't waiting for an answer.

"As for me?" I said. "All I want to do is keep looking for Gabe. That's all I'm thinking about. You already got me sidelined from it once. I'm not going to let that happen again, Kahlil. So unless you got something to say, I'm going to keep on rolling here."

I seriously expected him to hit me. So I was kind of surprised when he didn't. And of course, I wasn't going to give him time to change his mind, either, so I stepped around him and started moving up the hall.

I knew it wasn't the final word with me and Kahlil. In fact, that was kind of my point. Maybe he'd just keep coming for me as long as we were in the same school. It was like he couldn't help it. The same way I can't help being the way I am.

Or maybe I'm all wrong about that. I guess the point is, I just didn't care anymore. I could spend my time sweating over Kahlil, or I could focus on something that actually felt worth worrying about.

Guess which one I chose?

CHAPTER 37

WHEN I LEFT school, I knew I was going to be letting myself into the house. Nana was in court with Dad that day, and Jannie had track practice. So I wasn't in any big hurry to get there.

First, I spent some time handing out more flyers in front of school. Not too many people were interested in talking to me, but I was used to that by now. I just kept walking up and down E Street, giving them to whoever would take them, and asking as many people as I could if they'd seen Gabe in the last three weeks. Of course, the answer to that one was no, *no,* and more no.

After that, I took the bus to St. Anthony's Church. The truth was, I was getting desperate. I'm not that kid who says his prayers every single night. But sometimes when you run out of ways to hope for something, praying is the only thing left. I figured I might as well give it a shot.

Father Bernadin wasn't around, but the sanctuary was open. The last time I'd been there was Christmas Eve, when I had the whole congregation putting in a prayer for Gabe. This time, I stuck to the back. There were people near the front with their heads down, and I didn't want to bother them.

I slid into one of the last pews, got down on the kneeler, and bowed my head.

"Dear God," I whispered, keeping this one just between the two of us. "Thank you for making sure Gabe Qualls is okay so far. Please keep watching over him, and if there's anything you can do to help bring him home again, please do that, too."

I stopped and looked up for a second. Everything was so quiet in that church. It reminded me why people say God is always listening, and I hoped they were right.

Then I put my head down again and kept going. "I'm not sure what you think about Mr. Qualls, God, but if there's anything you can do to give him a better heart, or...I don't know...just make sure he's not a problem for Gabe, I'd really appreciate that, too."

I wasn't even sure what I was praying for anymore. I didn't want to ask for something bad to happen to Gabe's dad. I just wanted things to be okay for Gabe. Hopefully, God knew where I was coming from, even if I wasn't using the right words.

"Anyway," I whispered into my hands, "thank you for listening, and for everything you've done, and especially for anything you can do to help. I miss Gabe more and more every day..."

I stopped again, because I got this weird sensation. It's like when you can just *feel* someone's eyes on you. And then when I looked up, sure enough—

"Nana?"

She was standing right there in her coat, holding her purse like she was on her way out of the church.

I guess she'd been one of the people at the front, and I hadn't even noticed.

"What are you doing here?" I asked.

"Praying for your father," Nana Mama said. "But I might ask you the same question."

"Same thing," I said, because I was embarrassed that I hadn't thought about that. "And for Gabe, too."

"You know what?" Nana slid into the pew next to me. "Let's say one for Mr. Yang, while we're at it."

So I kept my head down, and let Nana take the lead on that one. Then I said amen with her at the end, and we got up to go. I'd kind of been hoping to do even more canvassing on my way home, but I put that idea on hold.

"Where are Dad and Bree?" I asked once we got outside.

"They both had to go back to work. We'll see them at home later," Nana told me. "How about we get some takeout from Lola's for dinner? I'm too pooped to cook after that day in court."

Nana even called an Uber, which is about as rare as hen's teeth, as she likes to say. She usually walks

241

everywhere, and the truth is, she's kind of cheap about that stuff. But I was tired, too, and I love the burgers from Lola's. So yeah, no complaints from me.

"How'd it go?" I asked once we were in the car, heading home. "At the trial, I mean."

Nana swiped at the air, like she was swatting away a mosquito. "That prosecutor is only interested in one thing: *winning*," she said. "But the truth will rise to the top. I have no doubt about that. I say your father can't lose."

I didn't know if she was just trying to make me feel better, but I liked that she said that. I needed some kind of good news.

"How are you feeling about Gabriel?" Nana Mama asked.

I shrugged, because I wasn't sure what to say.

"I just wish those detectives would move on Mr. Qualls already," I said. "I don't even know if they're talking to him, or what."

"Oh, honey," Nana said. "People in your dad's line of work have to keep a lot of secrets. You must know that by now. It doesn't mean they're sitting on their behinds."

"Still, why is it taking so long?" I asked.

Nana patted my hand while the Uber crawled through traffic. "Have a little faith, sweetheart," she said. "Try to trust in the process."

"Yeah, okay," I said. "I'll try."

And I really would. But it wasn't going to be easy.

ALEX CROSS

AFTER A LONG day in court, Alex Cross found himself jumping right back into work. Unofficially, anyway. He'd exchanged a few texts with Detective Olayinka through the afternoon, and now found himself in the backseat of Olayinka's blue Kia, headed south and east from the courthouse. Detective Sutter sat next to Olayinka in the front.

Word was, the police lab had found a match for William Qualls's fingerprints on Ali's school ID card. That was more than enough to justify another visit to the Qualls's house.

"Thanks for waiting to the end of the day," Alex told the detectives. "I appreciate your bringing me in on this."

"It's just a ride-along," Olayinka said, not for the first time. "You're still on non-contact status, Alex, and I need you to stay by the car when we get there."

"Of course," Alex said. He wasn't sure he trusted himself with what he'd do, anyway. What kind of grown man tried to frame a kid Ali's age? Probably the same kind who would use his own son as a pawn, and send him through a dog door to break into a house. That was the theory, anyway, though it didn't explain where Gabe Qualls had been all this time.

Everything was up in the air at this point, but Alex could feel it in his gut. They were getting closer to some answers here.

"How'd the trial go today?" Sutter asked while they traveled.

"No comment," Alex said. "Honestly, I'm exhausted, but hearing from you was the first piece of good news I've had, so I'll take it."

For the rest of the drive, they talked about the weather and the upcoming Super Bowl instead, until Olayinka was parking in front of a sad-looking row house on 17th Street. Alex got out of the car but kept himself on the sidewalk as the other two went to knock on the door. He wanted William Qualls to see him when he answered.

It took several knocks before anything happened. Sutter seemed to hear some kind of disturbance inside. "Mr. Qualls?" she called through. "It's Detective Sutter from MPD. Can you please open the door?"

Then, sure enough, William Qualls was there, looking out of breath. Alex couldn't hear the conversation, but Qualls's eyebrows knitted together at whatever they were telling him.

Yeah, that's right, Alex thought. *No more messing with kids' lives. It's time to answer to the grown-ups.*

After a few moments on the stoop, the detectives moved inside and the door closed behind them. Alex stuck to his spot, watching for maybe three or four minutes before anything else happened.

When he caught some movement through the cracked first-floor window, Alex stood up a little straighter, squinting in that direction. Then without warning, the window itself shattered as a large ashtray came through the glass and broke into a million pieces of its own on the pavement outside.

"What the...?"

Alex was already moving up the front walk when the door flew open. Inside, he could see Sutter on one knee. Blood was dripping through her fingers, where she had a hand up to her forehead. Behind her, Olayinka seemed to be helping Mrs. Qualls off the ground. A shattered picture frame was next to her where she'd gone down.

There was no time for questions, much less explanations. Even as Alex approached the house, Qualls burst out the door. He cleared the front steps in one leap, lowered his shoulder, and plowed right through Alex like J. J. Watt on a good day. Alex flew back and hit the pavement hard. By the time he'd scrambled onto his feet, Qualls was through the gate and sprinting up 17th Street at a good clip.

"Stop him!" Olayinka shouted from inside.

Alex took off running.

ALEX CROSS

QUALLS DIDN'T LOOK back, and he was no slouch on his feet, either. The guy could move. He had a good half block on Alex, but it was also true that Jannie Cross had inherited her long and fast legs from her dad.

Alex kept his chin down but his eyes on Qualls as he flew across F Street without even checking for traffic. A white SUV blared its horn, and a taxi's tires screeched on the pavement to avoid running Qualls down. He dodged a mother with a stroller, then a bale of newspapers on the sidewalk, and kept on sprinting.

Alex did the same, matching him stride for stride.

Massachusetts Avenue was the next cross street coming up, with a much busier intersection than the last one—hopefully enough to slow Qualls down. But Qualls may have been thinking the same thing. With less than twenty feet between them now, he suddenly cut to the right, off 17th and down a side alley. He snagged a household dumpster with one hand as he made the turn, and flung it in Alex's way. The can tipped. Garbage scattered onto the pavement.

Alex didn't see it coming fast enough. His shin barked against the edge of the bin. He lurched forward and sprawled onto the ground, but even then, momentum was on his side. Alex rolled without stopping, and was back on his feet a second later, in time to see Qualls turning another corner.

He'd gone down a second alley now, one that ran behind the houses on 17th. And this one was a dead end, Alex saw, as soon as he got there. It seemed like good news, until Qualls took a running leap onto someone's tall wooden back fence.

Boards cracked under the man's weight. He tipped back, but compensated with a swing of his leg up and over the fence, then fell onto the other side. By the time Alex was up and over the same fence, Qualls was furiously trying to kick through the back door of someone's house. It wasn't giving way, though, and Qualls was clearly cornered.

He seemed to know it, too. It showed in the fierce look that blazed in his eyes, a fraction of a second before he charged again, straight at Alex.

This time, Alex was ready. He feinted left as Qualls came, and threw an elbow into the other man's side.

"Get out of my yard!" someone screamed through a window. "I'm calling the police!"

"Good!" Alex yelled back. "And tell them to hurry!"

It wasn't over yet. Qualls scrambled out of Alex's grip, and tried to make another run for it. The only way out was over the fence, which was splintered and broken now, making for an awkward climb. There was no good place to grab on, and when Qualls tried, Alex was right there to pull him back.

Qualls whirled around and threw a punch, but missed.

It was his last mistake. As Qualls whiffed the punch, Alex saw another opening. He threw a left hook and connected with Qualls's exposed temple. His fist exploded with pain as he made contact, but Qualls got the worst of it. His whole body pivoted with a jerk and he dropped to the ground.

This time he didn't get up. Alex's handcuffs were off of his belt already, and he snapped the bracelets onto Qualls's wrists behind his back.

"William Qualls, you're under arrest. You have the right to remain silent..." Alex started to say, until he realized Qualls wasn't hearing any of it. He was out cold. And even if he did wake up, he wasn't going anywhere now.

Not until the cruiser arrived to take him away, once and for all.

CHAPTER 38

DAD TEXTED BREE to say he was going to be late for dinner that night, but I didn't find out why until he got home. And when I did...

Talk about a bombshell.

I was watching *The Incredibles 2* with Nana (she likes to keep it clean) when I heard the back door open. I was off the couch in a blink and ran into the kitchen to hear about Dad's day in court.

What I didn't expect—like in a million years— was to find Sutter and Olayinka standing there with him. Not only that, but the sleeve of Dad's jacket was half ripped off, his shirt was all dirty, and his tie was just plain gone. He was holding a bag of ice against his bloody knuckles, too.

"Dad? What happened?" I asked.

It turned out Nana was right. Sutter and Olayinka hadn't been holding back on this investigation at all. I guess Mr. Qualls bugged out when they showed up at his door. He'd clocked Detective Sutter with an ashtray—she was wearing a big gauze bandage on her forehead now—and he'd knocked down Mrs. Qualls, too, just before he made a run for it.

That's where Dad came in. He'd been the one to apprehend Mr. Qualls, which explained why he looked the way he did. Now Mr. Qualls was in a holding cell downtown, and it sounded like he'd already admitted to a whole bunch of stuff.

The house burglaries were something he'd started putting in place just after Thanksgiving. All he'd tell the cops was that he'd been picking out locations—starting with our house, since Gabe knew how to get in and out of there pretty easily. Just like I suspected.

According to Mr. Qualls, he'd sent Gabe to live with his half-brother, Ramon. The two of them were responsible for the actual break-ins, and for gathering together all the stuff they'd be selling to make money for the family. The whole idea was for Ramon to find a place for them to live, and to store their stolen goods, without Mr. Qualls ever knowing where any of that was going on. He was like the boss, while Ramon and Gabe did all the legwork. Then, if the cops came after Mr. Q—which they had—he wouldn't be able to turn his sons in, even if he wanted to. Because he didn't know where they were. But his big mistake was planting my ID at the scene of the last burglary. Because his fingerprints directly connected him to that crime, whether he actually committed it or not.

It wasn't such a bad plan, to be honest. I guess even Mrs. Qualls was in the dark, since he'd been lying to her, too. She really thought Gabe had run away, and she didn't know anything about the robberies. I wondered what she was thinking now, and how she was doing.

I wasn't sure why Gabe had agreed to do it in the first place, but my guess was that Mr. Qualls had threatened him so he didn't have a choice. It wasn't like that family had a ton of money, and my bet was that Gabe's TV, PS4, and some other stuff in the Qualls's house hadn't exactly come from Best Buy.

Meanwhile, the question nobody was answering yet was the one I most wanted to know: *Where was Gabe now?*

"Did Gabe ever mention this brother to you?" Detective Sutter asked. "Ramon Qualls?"

"Ramon?" I asked. "Yeah, I've heard of him, but I don't know anything about him."

I didn't admit that I only knew Ramon's name from the time I'd sneaked onto Bree's Accurint account. It wasn't like that made a difference, so I kept it to myself.

"What happens now?" I asked.

"That brings us to why we're here," Sutter told me.

She explained that Gabe was still in the dark. He needed to know it was safe to come home again, and that he wouldn't be charged for the robberies, or anything else his dad and Ramon had been forcing him to do.

"He'll be what's called a respondent in the case, not a defendant," Sutter told me. "The Attorney General's Office will have the authority to send him back to live with his mom, as long as Mr. Qualls is out of the picture. But meanwhile, Gabe doesn't know any of that."

"Okay?" I asked. I still didn't get what this had to do with me.

"We want to leave a message for Gabe inside that gaming system of yours," Sutter told me.

"In *Outpost*?" I asked.

"It's possible that's how his father has been communicating with him and Ramon," Olayinka said. "We found a second PS4 in Mr. and Mrs. Qualls's bedroom. And if we're right about this, that means Gabe will be checking in there on a regular basis."

I knew gaming consoles were forensically trackable that way. But it was also true that those kinds of messages didn't leave a digital footprint the way texting and emailing did. It made sense. It was pretty smart, actually.

"Yeah, I'll do it," I said. "But only on one condition. Ruby, Cedric, and Mateo need to be there, too."

"This isn't a negotiation, Ali," Sutter said.

"No, it's not," I said. "Because like I just told you, I won't do it without them. Those guys have been in on this from the beginning. They deserve to know about this just as much as me."

I think that part surprised the adults as much as I surprised myself. And if I was bluffing—because basically, I was—they didn't need to know that yet. I was going to do this for them either way. But first I wanted an answer.

"Actually," Olayinka said, "Gabe might be more likely to show up if he sees more of his friends logged on."

I wasn't sure that was true, but I liked getting Olayinka on my side. Dad wasn't saying anything either way, so now it was down to Detective Sutter.

"Yeah, yeah, okay," she said. "But only if they can do it right now. I'm not going to wait on this."

"Deal," I said. And a second later, I had my phone out, punching in a group text as fast as I could.

ME: You guys, listen to me. GET ONTO OUTPOST RIGHT NOW. Forget everything else that happened. If you care about Gabe's case, I swear, you need to be on here. Meet me at his bunker. The code is QUBUQ. I'm here with the police and we have to move on this right away!

Chapter 39

In the basement, I set Sutter up with the spare headset and ran it through the splitter I used when Cedric or Gabe came over to game with me. Then I logged in to *Outpost* and got us moving.

"This shouldn't take long," I said.

"Where are we headed?" Olayinka asked. "Which sector?"

I looked over at him. "You play *Outpost*?"

"Sure," he said. "Just leveled up my body armor with the new adaptive camo."

It was like every time I turned around, I learned something new about these detectives.

"Well, we have to get over to Gabe's compound in the northeast quadrant, fourth sector," I said.

"And you've been there before, right?" Olayinka asked. "So you can—"

"Fast travel," I said. "Yeah. This should just take a second. Hopefully our friends are going to show up, too."

Sure enough, when we got there, Cedric, Ruby, and Mateo were already waiting inside the bunker on the ground level. Or, at least, their avatars were.

"Hey!" I said. "That was quick."

"I was already playing when you texted," Cedric said. "I mean...you know. We were playing."

If it were any other time, it would have hurt my feelings to know they were gaming without me. But not today. It's called *bigger fish to fry*.

"This is crazy," Cedric said. "Like we're actually looking for Gabe *inside* the game."

"I don't know what to look for, but if he's logged on, he'll see we're all here," Ruby said.

"Here, in the bunker?" Mateo asked.

"Duh. Where do you *think* he'd be?" Cedric asked.

"Hey, you guys?" I said.

"How would I know?" Mateo asked.

"I'm just asking, fool," Cedric told him.

"You're the fool, fool," Mateo said, and they cracked up in my ear.

"Guys!" I tried again. "We've got Detective Sutter listening in with us, okay? Try to act like this is serious—'cause it is."

"Oh!" Cedric said. "Sorry, Ms. Sutter. Or... ma'am... or..."

"I think you mean Detective," Ruby said.

"No worries, guys," Sutter said, smiling over at me. "Let's get to this, okay?"

"This place is amazing," Olayinka said. He wasn't hearing the conversation but he could see Gabe's bunker on the screen.

"This is nothing," I said. "Hang on. Everyone follow me." And I led them to the back of the room, through the trap door, down the spiral stairs, and into the lower level.

"Whoa," Mateo said. "This is what I'm talking about."

"This kid's a genius," I heard Olayinka say under his breath. I couldn't help smiling at that, too. At least they were figuring out what they were dealing with here.

"And this is where he left me that note," I said, putting Cassius Play by the spot where I'd last seen it. "But it's gone now."

"That's good news," Olayinka told me. "That means Gabe's been here at least once more."

"So what happens now?" Ruby asked.

"Now, we leave him a note of our own," I told her, and turned to look at Detective Sutter again. "What do you want it to say?"

"I think you should each write one," she said.

"Cool," Mateo said.

"Really?" Ruby asked.

"Sure," Sutter said. "Ali, I'll work with you on yours, but the rest of you, just put it in your own words, and ask Gabe to come home or at least call 911 and check in."

"He's not in trouble?" Ruby asked.

"Not if his father's been compelling him to do

this," Sutter said. "Tell him that, too. He needs to know it's safe to come back."

Already, I was pulling down the main menu and choosing MESSAGE, then CUSTOM. I made it bright blue instead of yellow, so Gabe couldn't miss it.

It didn't take long to type in the message from there. *Outpost* had a keyboard app plug-in so I could use my phone for longer strings of text. Which is what I did.

ME: Gabe! I don't know how much you already know, but your dad was arrested tonight. He's not going back to your house, and I don't know if there's any way I can talk you into coming home, but you should DO IT. It's safe now, I promise. I'm working with the police.

ME: Ruby, Cedric, and Mateo are all here, too. I'm really sorry about opening it up like this. I know you asked me not to, but everything's changed now. Please, please, please come home. Or at least hit us back up here. We can work something out. I know we can. You're safe.

ME: Your friend, Ali

CHAPTER 40

THE NEXT DAY was day two of Dad's trial, but once again, I wasn't allowed to be there. I had to go to school and try to focus on other things. Lucky for me (if you can call it "lucky"), I had the Gabe stuff to work on.

And even better, I was back in with Ruby, Mateo, and Cedric. I got to eat lunch with them that day, which was a huge relief.

I was right about Ruby, too. She hadn't stopped working on this case for a minute. Now we had more than twenty kids signed up to go looking for

Gabe after school, block by block, handing out flyers, knocking on doors, and working in teams.

I knew Dad didn't want us investigating Gabe's disappearance anymore, but there was no rule against talking to people and asking if they'd seen a missing kid. Or, at least, that's what I told myself. Because there was no stopping us now. Even Ruby and Mateo's parents had gotten on board. As long as they partnered up with someone and got home by five thirty, they were allowed to get out there with us.

I'd brought my map of DC to school, and we were all looking at it now while we ate.

"So you said somewhere between 14th and 17th, he turned off of E Street," Ruby said. She had the map folded back to the line of yellow highlighter I'd drawn over Gabe's route from school to home.

"Yeah," I said, using a French fry to point at the three-block stretch she was talking about. We were going to start from Wash-Latin, so that was just two blocks down from where we were already.

"But here's what I was thinking," she said, looking up again with that Ruby look in her eye. The one that said *I'm as smart as anyone, so bring it.* "You also told us Gabe was begging you to stop looking for him, right?"

"Right."

"And these robberies. They've all been pretty near your house, right?"

"Keep going," I said.

"See, I think maybe we're focusing on the wrong neighborhood," Ruby said. "Actually, let me put that another way. I think maybe we're asking ourselves the wrong question."

"Huh?" Cedric said, and I was kind of with him on that.

"What do you mean?" I asked Ruby. "What's the right question?"

"The right question is, *why* was Gabe so concerned about you not looking for him?" Ruby answered.

"Because he didn't want to get caught," I said.

"Yeah," she said. "But maybe that's only half the answer."

"Just tell us what you mean, already," Mateo said.

Ruby leaned in again and ran her finger across the map, from our school, over to where my house was on 5th Street.

"Maybe he was afraid that if you looked hard enough, you'd actually be able to find him," she said. "And maybe that means he's hiding out somewhere close by where you live."

We all let that sink in for a minute.

On the one hand, Gabe could have been anywhere. On the other hand, Ruby was making some sense. Also, we had to pick something to run with, or we'd never get anywhere. Just like in *Outpost*.

"I like it," I said.

Ruby nodded and sat back. "Right? Let's stop thinking about where Gabe was last seen and start thinking about where we know he's been since then."

"Like in Ali's hood," Mateo said.

"Exactly," Ruby said.

Mateo had a sign-up sheet for all the other canvassing volunteers, and he pulled it out now. "I'll tell everyone else and start making assignments."

"Awesome," Cedric said. "I mean, I didn't really follow all that, but whatever. I'm in. We got a real operation here, don't we?"

And he was right. We really did.

CHAPTER 41

IT WAS PRETTY great, having so many kids pair up and cover my neighborhood after school that day. For about an hour and a half, it was like we were everywhere you looked.

I went with Mateo, Ruby went with Cedric, and we all knocked on as many doors as we could before people had to start cutting out. It didn't get us any new leads, but at the same time, it just felt good to cover so much ground.

When I got home, the first thing I did was check

Gabe's bunker. All of our messages were still there, but that didn't mean Gabe hadn't seen them. He could have easily read them and left them where they were. Either way, he hadn't responded.

And then late that night, the four of us were back at it. Not knocking on doors, but group texting and brainstorming, thinking about next moves.

MATEO: You think Gabe's brother has an apartment around here?

ME: Don't know. Not in his name anyway, or the cops would have found it.

MATEO: I'm thinking maybe some old abandoned place or something.

RUBY: Under the highway? Over by the tracks? Maybe in the park?

ME: Nah. Too cold out. Also, if he has PS4, he has electricity.

CEDRIC: And internet.

RUBY: Could be hacking in somewhere. Or using a hotspot.

MATEO: I'll bet he is. But WHERE???

ME: We just gotta keep trying. I say we stick to this neighborhood for now.

CEDRIC: Totally.

MATEO: I'm down.

RUBY: Okay.

All of a sudden, while I was sitting there going back and forth with my friends, I heard Dad's ringtone, coming from up in the attic. It was quarter to twelve by now. That could only mean one thing—some kind of police business. And I wanted to know what it was.

Hang on. I think something's happening. Be right back.

Then I pulled one of my usual moves. I got out of bed, snuck over to the door, out into the hall, and took a position. This time, I put myself at the bottom of the attic stairs, where I could hear Dad talking in his office. I didn't know what was up yet, but my gut told me something was about to change, all over again.

ALEX CROSS

ALEX CROSS SPENT several more hours at his desk that night, mostly worrying about the trial.

Day two had been another long haul, this one devoted to his defense. Deirdre Tennant had called a city engineer to tell how the Yangs' front steps hadn't been built to code, and a doctor from Mr. Yang's medical team to emphasize what had already been established about Mr. Yang's bruises following his accident. None of it was a slam dunk, but it helped, anyway.

Now it was just a waiting game for the verdict. Alex had tried to put on a good game face during dinner that night, but it was hard not to worry. The whole family was on edge, and for good reason. This time tomorrow Alex would be looking at a guilty verdict and a jail sentence—or he wouldn't. The jury could go either way.

So when a call came in from Isaac Olayinka late that night, it was a welcome distraction. Alex's first guess before he answered was that Gabriel Qualls had finally turned up, but he also knew how unpredictable these things could be.

"Hey," he answered.

"You're not going to believe this," Olayinka told him. "Or maybe you will."

"They found him," Alex said.

"Nope. Another robbery," Olayinka said. "Three, actually. I'm thinking Ramon Qualls is stepping up to the plate. Either that, or his dad had these in the hopper ahead of time. But in any case, we aren't done yet."

"What do we know about this Ramon kid, anyway?" Alex asked. He started googling the name as they spoke, but it didn't turn up much.

"He's twenty years old, and his last known residence is in Baltimore, but he hasn't been seen there since August," Olayinka said. "As a juvenile, he was in and out of the system since he was twelve, with a long record to show for it."

"Where are you?" Alex asked. "I'll come by if it's okay."

"Closer than ever," Olayinka said. "F Street Terrace, number 529."

"529 F Street Terrace," Alex repeated back. "Got it. I'll see you in a few."

"You really don't have to," Olayinka said. "There's nothing that needs doing. Just thought you might want to know."

"Yeah, well, it beats sitting around here not getting any sleep."

"Why? You waiting on a verdict tomorrow?" Olayinka asked.

The answer was yes, but Alex's trial was the last thing he wanted to talk about right now.

"I shouldn't be more than a few minutes," he answered, and hung up the phone.

CHAPTER 42

I **PUT THE** address in my phone as soon as I heard Dad say it, so I wouldn't forget.

529 F Street Terrace.

Then I went back to my room, changed out of my sweats super quick, and waited for Dad to come down.

I sat just inside my door until I heard his feet on the stairs. He went from the attic to the second floor, and then straight down to the front door. I heard him putting on his coat. Then the door opened and closed behind him.

Another second later, I was sneaking down the stairs, grabbing my own coat, and heading out the back of the house. If another robbery had gone down, that meant Gabe might still be out here on the street somewhere. It was the best chance I'd had for spotting him since he returned my laptop. I wasn't going to pass this up.

Meanwhile, it made sense to go the long way around. If Dad spotted me, I'd probably be grounded for life. I didn't need to tail him, anyway. I knew where F Street Terrace was. Really, I just wanted to get a look at this crime scene before I started doing what I'd come outside to do.

From behind our house, I walked down to Virginia Avenue, then around to 6th Street, up to G, and over to F Street Terrace. That gave Dad plenty of time to get there first. And even then, I hung on the corner in the dark, keeping out of sight.

The house was maybe halfway up the street. A couple of cop cars were parked out front, where I could see the door was wide open. An evidence response van was just pulling up from the opposite direction, and my guess was that Dad had already gone inside.

Not that it mattered. This was just my starting point, the one place I could assume Gabe had been tonight. So I pulled my hat out of my pocket and jammed it down on my head. Then I turned away and started walking.

When I came to the next corner, I took a left. Then at the next corner, I took another left. And again at the next one. This was a thing I'd read about, for searching a neighborhood as efficiently as possible. Once I'd come all the way around the block, I kept going until I came to a new left turn I hadn't already taken. And it went on like that, in a big spiral, always covering new ground.

I was scanning the whole time, too, checking the fronts of houses, the side alleys, the street ahead of me, and the street behind. There was never any knowing where Gabe might be, so I tried to stay as sharp as possible.

My best guess was that he had gone nocturnal, lying low during the day and coming out at night to do these jobs—the ones he'd been forced to do. First by Mr. Qualls, and now, from the sound of it, by his half-brother Ramon.

Walking around the neighborhood by myself in the middle of the night like this was the most dangerous thing I'd done yet. But the weird part was, I didn't care. I wasn't even scared, although maybe I should have been.

But nothing was as important as this. And that meant nothing was going to stop me from trying to put eyes on Gabe while I had the chance.

CHAPTER 43

THE FULL TRUTH is, I didn't really expect to find Gabe. I knew it was a crazy long shot.

So when it actually happened, you might say I was as surprised as I've ever been in my life.

I was walking up 7th Street, about halfway up the block, when I spotted him. Or, at least, *someone*. It was a small shadow of a person, holding a white plastic garbage bag, and that was all the clue I needed. I could tell just from the size of that shadow that it was him. And as for the garbage bag, that was exactly how we'd gotten back our stuff on the night Gabe returned it.

Gabe!

His name was just about to come out of my mouth when something stopped me. The part of my brain that listened to Dad about being a good detective said, *wait.* Maybe it made more sense to see what he did, and where he went after that.

I hung back again. I kept my eyes glued on his every move as he walked up the steps of a house in the middle of the block, carrying something heavy in that bag. It was like déjà vu, but from a different angle.

When he got to the door, he looked up and down the street one more time. I ducked behind a tree, just in case, although it was pretty dark out there.

By the time I was sneaking another look, Gabe was already ringing the bell. Then, just as fast, he dropped the bag, flew back down the stairs, and started running.

I still didn't want to yell his name, so I ran after him instead, keeping my distance. If he knew I was there and then managed to ditch me, for whatever reasons of his own, I'd be back to square one. But if I could figure out where he was going, that would put me a whole lot closer to solving this thing, once and for all.

I hung back as far as I could, and marked the way Gabe turned at the bottom of the block. Then I sprinted to the corner and just caught sight of him turning again, this time onto 6th Street. There was only one thing down that way—the underpass that ran underneath the interstate.

It made sense. There were plenty of places to hide out on the other side of the highway. And in fact, it was exactly the way I'd guessed he might have run on that night when he returned my laptop. I kept on tailing him, and kept my mouth shut for the time being. Because something told me wherever Gabe was headed right now, it wasn't going to be very far away.

CHAPTER 44

I COULDN'T GET too close, but I couldn't let him get too far away, either. Once Gabe walked into the dark of the underpass, I slipped in there behind him. Car noises overhead gave me some cover, but there were no streetlights now, either. It was easy not to be seen.

At the far side, he kept going. There were a ton of construction sites on that side of the highway, and I wondered if maybe Gabe and Ramon were crashing in some half-finished building.

But it wasn't that. Less than a block later, he stopped at a chain-link fence and pulled a corner of it back from the post holding it up. Inside, there was a big four-story building, with a RE-STORE DEPOT sign on the side.

It was all storage units, as far as I could tell. Was this where he'd been staying? It was weird, but not out of the question. In fact, it was starting to make sense.

I watched Gabe cross the parking lot on the other side of the fence. Then I pulled back the same piece of chain link and squeezed through. Gabe was just disappearing around the corner of the building, so I ran as quietly as I could up to that corner and stopped again.

I listened. At first there was nothing. Then just a small sound, like metal against metal.

I decided to risk another look. And there he was, kneeling in front of one of the ground floor units. These were the big kind where people keep cars and trucks, with a garage door that rolls straight up. Gabe was unlocking a padlock at the bottom.

A second later, he had the lock off and raised the

door. It seemed really loud from where I was, but then again, nobody was around to hear it. The only other real noise was coming from the highway.

As I moved around the corner, a light came on from inside Gabe's unit. It spilled onto the concrete, and I could hear him moving around in there. So I could conclude no one else was in there, unless they were sitting in the dark.

Just like that, I was out of reasons for hanging back. I'm not even sure why I was so nervous, but I guess it was time to find out, one way or another.

I walked over to the door, which was only open about three feet. Then I ducked down, stepped inside, and stood up again.

It was like a big garage in there. Or a tiny apartment. The place was jammed with stuff that looked like it had been taken from people's houses. There were TVs, computers, a few bikes, and a bunch of different boxes all over the floor. They also had wire shelving units with smaller electronics, luggage, jewelry boxes, and I couldn't even tell what else.

Closer to the front, they had two sleeping bags

on foam pads on the floor. Next to each one was a TV with its own PlayStation hooked up. And I guess they had power, too, because there was a mini fridge, a couple of space heaters, and some clip lights mounted on the wall.

The weirdest part was, it looked a whole lot like the storage room Gabe had designed for his bunker in *Outpost*. Obviously, this one didn't have a secret trap door down to a real apartment, but it was pretty clear where Gabe had gotten the inspiration for the rest. He'd probably been spending his days in that storage unit, waiting to go out at night, and playing two tons of *Outpost* in the meantime. It was like it all made sense, all at once.

"Gabe?" I finally said.

He yelled and spun around. When he saw me, his eyes popped and his jaw dropped open. I could tell he couldn't believe what he was seeing.

"Sorry," I said. "Don't be scared."

He stayed right where he was. I couldn't even tell if he was glad to see me.

"W-what are you doing here?" he stuttered.

"Duh," I said. "Looking for you. Did you get our messages?"

"Yeah," he said.

"Why didn't you answer? You need to come home, Gabe. It's safe, now."

"Nah," he said. "It's not. And you've gotta go. *Right now.*"

"Hang on," I said. He was walking toward me, looking like he was actually going to push me right out of there, but then he stopped again.

"What is it?" I asked.

He wasn't looking at me anymore. He was looking behind me. And when I turned around, another guy was standing there. This dude was older, like maybe Jannie or Damon's age, wearing jeans and a black Under Armour hoodie, with new Jordan Retro Fours on his feet.

I didn't recognize him, but I knew right away who it was. *Ramon Qualls.* And he was looking at me like I was just some trash that needed to be taken out.

CHAPTER 45

"WHAT DO YOU think you're doing here?" Ramon asked. He rolled the door shut behind him and the sound of it clanging into the cement made me flinch.

I was cornered, obviously. I just wasn't sure how scared I needed to be. Gabe wouldn't let Ramon do something *really* bad to me, would he?

At the same time, this guy was nobody to mess with, I could tell. He was big like their father. And he was wearing a big backpack, too. Probably full of whatever he'd just taken from someone's house.

"You're Ramon, right?" I said. "I'm not here to make trouble."

"I think you are," Ramon said, and took a step toward me.

"Bro, just keep cool," Gabe said. "He's not going to turn us in."

But Ramon kept coming. "Yeah, see, I don't buy that," he told me. "You're the one Gabe was talking to that night, aren't you?"

"Yeah," I admitted.

"So you already know too much," he said. "You're also the cop's kid."

I didn't answer, but I didn't have to. He knew.

"You shouldn't have come here," Ramon told me. He took another step forward.

I tried not to show how much I was shaking, but I also didn't know what this guy might do to me. I'd been scared of Mr. Qualls, for sure, but I never thought he'd *really* hurt me. Not in a big way. But with Ramon? It felt different, like all bets were off.

Especially since nobody even knew where I was. And he probably knew that.

"I'm sorry," I whispered. "I can just go. I won't tell."

But Ramon was already on me. He twisted me around and pulled my arm up behind my back, then pushed me into the ground.

"Ow! Get off!" I couldn't help yelling out. I thought he was about to snap my elbow.

"Ramon, get off him, man! Stop!" Gabe was yelling.

I could feel Ramon behind me, but I couldn't see him. My face was pressed into cold ground now, and the concrete was digging right into my cheek.

Then I heard Ramon's voice by my ear. "You don't even know what kind of mistake you just made. Now we gotta clear everything out of here, and..." He pushed my face a little harder into the ground. "I ain't happy about it."

I felt a punch in my side then, and the air rushed out of me.

"Stop it!" Gabe yelled.

"We're going to need a truck," Ramon said next, like it was some kind of business as usual.

"Don't worry," Gabe told him. "It's cool, man. It really is. He was just making sure I was all right. Ali won't tell—"

"I won't!" I cried. "Just get off me!"

When I struggled, he yanked my arm even harder. It really did feel like it was going to break. My eyes watered from the pain and I didn't have any choice but to stay still.

"Gabe, get outside," Ramon said.

"No!"

"Gabe..." Ramon said. Now I felt something else against my neck. Something metal and cold, with an edge. "Don't make this worse than it has to be. Now *get outside* before I start taking pieces off your friend here."

"Okay, okay!" I heard Gabe. "I'm going." Then I heard the door roll open again and felt a rush of cold air.

Finally, Ramon took his knee off my back. I whipped around and he was still standing over me. I could see the knife in his hand, too. And the look in his eyes. It reminded me of Mr. Qualls.

"Give me your phone," he said. "Now!"

I didn't have any choice. I handed it over.

"We'll be back," he said. "And then you're going to help us pack up."

"What's going on?" I asked. "What are you doing?" I felt half out of my mind, and whatever Ramon saw on my face, he just laughed.

"Calm down, little dude. I'm not going to kill you. We're just going to pack up, go for a drive, and drop you off somewhere outside the city."

"Where?" I asked.

"I guess we'll both know when we get there," Ramon said.

"I'm sorry, Ali!" Gabe said. I couldn't see him outside in the dark, but I could hear him. "I tried to warn you."

It was true. He had. I'd thought he was warning me about Mr. Qualls, but there was more to it than that. I could see that now.

Ramon had backed up to the door, still holding his knife where I could see it. I wasn't stupid enough to try anything, so I stayed put.

"We'll be back," he said. "And trust me, little

dude. You mess with any of our stuff—seriously, one scratch—and I *will* cut you up."

"He means it," Gabe said. "Seriously, Ali. You'll be okay. Just sit tight."

Then Ramon reached over, pulled an extension cord, and the lights went out, just before he rolled the door closed and the whole place went pitch black.

"When are you coming back?" I yelled. But nobody answered. All I heard was the sound of Ramon clicking that padlock back into place and locking me inside.

As soon as I heard that, I scrambled onto my feet and lurched toward the door. But it was no good. I bumped into something hard and went down again. In fact, I couldn't see a single thing. Not even my hand in front of my face.

Oh, no.

No way.

This wasn't happening, I thought.

It couldn't be.

Except, of course, it *was*.

CHAPTER 46

FOR A WHILE, I just yelled. Screamed my guts out. But something told me it wasn't going to do any good, and Ramon knew that.

I started to panic then. I thought my eyes would adjust, until I realized there was nothing to adjust to. No light was getting in there, and I couldn't stop breathing too fast. I felt like I was blind.

I didn't know how to turn on the lights, either. I'd have to find that extension cord *and* the outlet, all the way on the other side of the room, behind stacks of boxes and other stuff.

It seemed like a long, long time before anything happened at all. I couldn't think straight, and I wasn't coming up with any kind of solution, or idea. Without my phone, I really was stuck.

I sat there and tried to think about everything I knew was right around me. Maybe something I could use to pry the door? Or some other way to get some light in there?

I was sitting on Gabe's sleeping bag now, and I tried to see it in my mind. What else was near me?

I started groping around. I put my hand on the sleeping bag, and felt my way up to the pillow. Then the cardboard box he'd been using like a table. I knocked over a bunch of empty cans.

Then my hand landed on something hard, like another box. *The TV.* That's what I was looking for. That, and Gabe's PS4. I didn't know how to turn on the TV, but I knew how to turn on the PlayStation.

I got up on my knees now. Hopefully I had time to do this. They'd be gone for a while, almost for sure. I figured the TV and PS4 were far enough away from the extension cord Ramon pulled that they probably weren't plugged into it. I felt around the back of the

TV, searching with my fingers for the flat, rubbery HDMI cable I knew would be there. When I found it, I kept going, hand over hand, along the cable like a rope, until I got to the console I was looking for.

The power button isn't easy to find on a PS4, if you don't know what you're doing. Lucky for me, I did. My fingers ran along the front of the console until I felt the little vertical rectangular sensor I was looking for. Gabe mentioned once that he mastered his PS4 to his TV, and sure enough, when I touched the sensor, the TV fired up, too. The ghostly glow lit up the whole storage area.

It was a huge relief to be able to see again, like taking a breath for the first time when your lungs are about to explode.

Now I could look for the controller, which was back by Gabe's sleeping bag. I snatched it up and started logging in as a guest right away. Then I put in my own username and password and went straight to *Outpost*.

From there, I started leaving messages for everyone I could. I even looked up Detective Olayinka. He'd told me that his screen name was IOIO522, and I found him right away. He had a sweet avatar, too, all decked out in dark-blue body armor, with LED eyes that glowed yellow.

But this was no time for avatars. I needed real people, and I left the same message for Cedric, Ruby, and Mateo, who were all probably asleep. If I was lucky, maybe Cedric would be up late.

Help! This is Ali. I'm locked in Gabe and Ramon's storage unit at a place called RE-STORE, near 6th and K by the highway. They're gone and I don't know where they are, but I need someone to come let me out. Is anyone there? I don't have a phone. Please come ASAP!!!!! And call my dad, too!

I included Dad's phone number, but I wasn't fooling myself. It was pretty late, and I didn't think anyone was going to see this until morning, at least. Even then, maybe not until later, since it was a school night.

I couldn't think about it too much. I'd done what I could.

The only thing left to do now was wait—and hope that Ramon Qualls didn't come back too soon.

CHAPTER 47

I DON'T KNOW how much time went by. It was maybe an hour. Maybe two. I kept getting scared, and then calming down. Then getting scared again.

I started screaming again, but without much hope. No one could—

BANG!

What was that? A gunshot? I dove down onto Gabe's sleeping bag.

"Ali!"

It was Dad's voice, and I practically exploded with relief. Or melted. Or both.

"Dad! Dad! Dad!" I was tripping on stuff just to get to the front. I didn't care. Then I was banging on the door. "I'm here! I'm here!"

"Hang on a second," he said.

"You have to cut the lock!" I yelled. "It's near the ground."

"No, we got this," Dad said.

Faster than I was expecting, I heard a rattle outside, and then Dad threw open the door. He was hugging me as fast as I was hugging him, and behind that, I could see Gabe standing there.

"Yo," he said. "I don't know what you want to say to me, but I'm really sorry. I just—"

Gabe didn't get any further than that. I was already hugging him next, and I didn't care what he thought about that.

"Thanks for not giving up on me," he said before I let go.

"I thought you wanted me to," I said, and stepped back.

"So did I. Until now," he said.

"Good thing I don't listen," I told him, and we both grinned, maybe because we were both trying not to cry.

"But listen, man," Gabe told me. "I never, ever should have gone into your house like that. It was way out of line."

"It's okay," I said. It really was.

"My pops was out of control," he kept going. "He told me we were going to lose the house if I didn't help out, and even when I told him that didn't mean I had to go crash with Ramon, he wasn't hearing it. Basically, I could stay home and get a beatdown when he felt like it, or I could get in the game."

"I know you didn't have a choice," I said. "I get it. It's really okay, Gabe. I promise."

Gabe wasn't even listening. The words were just kind of pouring out of him—which is something I could relate to. Sometimes you just have to say what you have to say, no matter what.

"You're like my only real friend, Ali, and I get it if you tell me we're done, after this. I think some of your family's stuff is still in here, but a lot of it got sold. I'll pay you back if I can—"

"Gabe!" I said. "Seriously, man. Don't worry about any of that. What I want to know is what just happened." I looked at Gabe, then Dad, then Gabe again. "How did you...I mean...why are you both here?"

"Cedric called my cell," Dad told me. "And a patrol officer nabbed Ramon Qualls when he was trying to steal a truck. It took a bit to get it sorted out, but Gabe brought me right to this unit."

That seemed like a pretty quick version of a longer story, but I just wanted to get out of there. I'd dig for details later. I could see two more patrol cars pulling into the parking lot through the gate and stopping next to Dad's car.

"Can we go?" I asked. "Please?"

"Of course," Dad said.

"Can Gabe come with us?" I asked.

"As far as his house," Dad told me. "His mom's expecting us."

"What about Ramon?" I asked as we walked to the car.

"Ramon's in custody," Dad said. "He'll be facing quite a few charges, I'm afraid."

Gabe was pretty quiet. I'm guessing the whole thing felt pretty complicated for him.

"I guess that means it's just me and my mom again," he said. "That's good. I guess."

"Nah. Not just you and your mom," I said, and even let him take the front seat when we got to Dad's car. "You got us, Gabe. You've always got us. Clear?"

Gabe just nodded at that. He wasn't ever very big with words to begin with. But I think he got where I was coming from. And if I had anything to say about it, he wasn't ever going to have another reason to leave home again.

CHAPTER 48

LATER THAT SAME morning, everyone in the family but Damon was at court for Dad's verdict. After everything that had happened, Dad and Bree both thought I should stay home with Nana. But that was before Nana and I both put a big *absolutely not* on that one.

Yeah, it had been a long, hard night, to say the least. But there was no way in the world I was going to be skipping Dad's verdict. And with Nana on my side, that was pretty much that.

I wore a tie, and Jannie dressed up, too. The suspense couldn't have been higher, while we sat there in chairs on the other side of the barrier from the defense table.

"Whatever happens, guys, we're going to be okay," Dad told us.

We all nodded like we knew that was true, but I wasn't so sure. I hadn't gotten a second of sleep, and even so, I was as wide awake as I could be.

Correction—when that judge walked into the courtroom and the jury started filing in, too, I got just a little more hyped. It was hard sitting still, not saying anything, and just waiting to hear what happened next.

"Would the defendant rise, please?" Judge Lautner asked. Dad and Ms. Tennant stood up. I thought we should, too, but Bree and Nana stayed in their seats, so I followed their lead. Jannie took my hand on one side, and I grabbed Nana's on the other.

"Madam foreman, have you reached a verdict?" she asked a lady in the first jury seat.

"We have, your honor."

The lady handed a piece of paper to the bailiff, who passed it over to the judge, before she read it and then turned back to the jury again.

"And how do you find?" the judge asked.

The lady stood up and read from another sheet in her hand. "In the matter of District of Columbia vs. Cross, we, the jury, find the defendant..."

It seemed like time stopped for a fraction of a second. My stomach squirmed.

"...*not guilty*," the forewoman said.

I think all the air rushed out of me at once. Then back in, as I took a huge breath. I knew my dad was a good person. I didn't need a judge and jury to tell me that. But still, I've never been so relieved in my life.

Nana had her arms around me now, and Jannie, too. Bree was hugging Dad, and then the whole bunch of us. For a second, I couldn't even see anything, and all I could hear was a little bit of crying. The happy kind.

"Very well," Judge Lautner said. "Ladies and gentlemen of the jury, thank you for your service. Dr.

Cross, might I just add that as far as I can tell from my own research, this has been an unfortunate detour in an exemplary career. I thank you for your service to this community as well. You are free to go."

Then she banged her gavel once. And just like that, it was over.

Chapter 49

WHEN WE GOT outside, there was more press than I'd seen in one place since this whole thing started. I saw cameras, and people with tape recorders, and a whole bunch of news vans with their towers up, parked out on Indiana Avenue.

"Here we go," Dad said, as we came down the steps and they all rushed toward us. "I'll keep it quick," he added.

I was so used to Dad no-commenting his way through this stuff, I was surprised he wanted to say anything at all. But I guess that's what usually happens after the trial.

He stood his ground this time, and let everyone come to him, until we were basically surrounded.

"How are you feeling, Alex?" someone asked.

"Tired," Dad said, and a few people laughed.

"Do you think justice was served, Detective Cross?" another reporter jumped in.

"In that I told the truth during my trial? Yes," Dad said.

"Meanwhile, reports of police brutality are up more than twenty percent," someone else said. "Do you think civilians have a good reason to be afraid of the police?"

For that one, Dad took his time. He waited until everyone had stopped clamoring, too.

"I think *some* civilians have good cause to be afraid of *some* police," he said. "There have been too many reports of unnecessary violence by officers in this country. That can't be ignored, and it shouldn't be. All I can do, as an officer of the law, is uphold my duties and responsibilities to keep our community as safe as I possibly can. I also know that people will think and say whatever they want about my case after this verdict. But I am pleased with the outcome of this trial, and I hope the Yang family can find some peace as they wait for Mr. Yang to recover."

"What's next, Alex?"

"I'm looking forward to getting back to work," Dad said. "I'll also be launching a GoFundMe campaign for Stanley Yang's family, if they'll accept it, to help them through this difficult time."

That was news to me, but it seemed like a great idea.

"Does that mean you still feel guilty, Alex?" a reporter asked.

"No," Dad said. "It just means I'm human. Today, I can start to put my life back together. But Stanley Yang is still in that hospital bed. And the one thing we can all agree on is that the Yang family deserves our prayers, as well as any help we can offer them."

I've always been proud of Dad, but it felt like my chest filled up with helium just then. I probably had a big dumb smile on my face, too.

There was another round of questions after that,

but Dad handed those off to Ms. Tennant so we could get out of there. Then, as we all headed to the car, it was like none of us had anything to say. Everyone was just quiet, which is pretty unusual for my family. Much less for me.

But meanwhile, inside my head, it was as noisy as ever. I was thinking about everything that had happened. And about Gabe. And my friends. And about Dad, too.

Mostly about Dad.

I don't know if I'll ever measure up to who he is, but I do know that someday I want to be as much like my father as I can. I want to go to Johns Hopkins like he did. I want to go to the police academy. And most of all, I want to be a real detective, just like him.

Which is a tall order, if you know anything about Alex Cross.

The fact is, I'm pretty small for my age. I don't know if I'll ever be as big as Dad, much less that strong, or brave. And I still have a *whole* lot to learn. Maybe I'll be as smart as him one day, and maybe I won't. I guess time will tell.

But meanwhile, I realized, there is one thing I don't have to wait for, or grow up for, or even change to make happen.

I don't have to wait to become a detective.

Because, see, I already am one.

About the Author

James Patterson received the Literarian Award for Outstanding Service to the American Literary Community from the National Book Foundation. He holds the Guinness World Record for the most #1 *New York Times* bestsellers, including *Max Einstein, Middle School, I Funny,* and *Jacky Ha-Ha,* and his books have sold more than 385 million copies worldwide. A tireless champion of the power of books and reading, Patterson created a children's book imprint, JIMMY Patterson Books, whose mission is simple: "We want every kid who finishes a JIMMY Book to say, 'PLEASE GIVE ME ANOTHER BOOK.'" He has donated more than three million books to students and soldiers, and funds more than four hundred Teacher and Writer Education Scholarships at twenty-one colleges and universities. He has also donated millions of dollars to independent bookstores and school libraries. Patterson invests proceeds from the sales of JIMMY Patterson Books in pro-reading initiatives.